Hoffman, Andy
Beehive

S 10/13/98

BEEHIVE

by Andy Hoffman

THE PERMANENT PRESS
Sag Harbor, New York 11963

Fiction

Library of Congress Cataloging-in-Publication Data

Hoffman, Andy, 1956–
   Beehive / Andy Hoffman.
      p.   cm.
   ISBN 1-877946-14-1 : $21.95
   I. Title.
   PS3558.O344745B44   1992
   813'.54—dc20   91-32974
                      CIP
Manufactured in the United States of America

THE PERMANENT PRESS
Noyac Road
Sag Harbor, NY 11963

For my father, who would have enjoyed this; for Judy, who does; and for Marcus, who will.

BEEHIVE

1.

I never meant to be a hero. What's more, I never was meant to be one either. That's more important. Of course, sometimes your own life veers out of control. Like with the bees. Sometimes a big wind blows up and knocks the hive over, or some inexperienced keeper will move the hive a couple yards to where they think they should have set it up to start with. But the bees don't have the same perspective as people, and when they go home and the hive has moved, they just buzz around where the hive used to be. They're not dumb, mind you; I think they're smarter than me, but that doesn't say much. They know home by the position of the sun and the hive's place in its surroundings.

Sooner or later, one of the bees might find the hive and convince the others to return to it, but that's extraordinary. Single bees aren't meant for that sort of heroic action. They have more intelligence as a hive than you could imagine from watching bees one by one. So this one bee who finds the hive never intended to do anything of the sort. All she knew was her home and her queen were missing, and she would never rest until she found them.

2.

I left the Bureau at my regular time, just after everyone else had gone home. I learned very early that diligence makes up for many shortcomings, especially in work. So few people have exceptional skills or consistently come up with new ideas that diligence becomes the only way to judge someone's work. Diligence or birthright. I don't have the latter, so I use the former, and it's worked so far. I'm Assistant Chief in the Housing Characteristics Division of the Bureau of the Census. One of the Assistant Chiefs in the Housing Characteristics Division, I should say.

I stay until six, usually. It takes an extra hour to fix the mistakes of the day anyway. The people I work with don't seem quite as diligent as me, but they all have children to raise and houses to tend and parents to care for, necessary obligations. I'm a civil servant, so I help them with their work. They wouldn't let me help rear their children, of course, so what can I do? We're all in this together. After all, where would America be if we let the children slip away because we were too busy with our jobs?

The phone machine blinked with two messages. The first was from Jim that morning, reporting he'd found two more supercedure cells in one of the hives. The second came from Elizabeth. "I won't be home tonight," she said. "The General has a meeting in Newport first thing tomorrow morning and decided he wanted me along. We're staying overnight on base. Lucky I picked up the cleaning on my way in today. I'll be back tomorrow."

3.

So I fired up the 'mobile and headed out to Virginia. See what I mean about heroes? If I had different parents, maybe I would have gotten drunk, or called up Jean, the programmer in Operations who always sends me messages. But I take Elizabeth at her word. I know her craziness about her work. And how can I blame her? A twenty-seven-year-old woman attached to the Joint Chiefs of Staff? She wants to be in the Cabinet before she's forty and I don't see how she can miss. She's ready now, as far as I can tell.

I met her eighteen months before, at a party I hardly expected to go to. A woman I had tried to help through a crisis—that's what I thought I was doing anyway—insisted I come to an embassy cocktail party. I know about these gatherings only from rumor. They hold them weekdays because people don't like to work on weekends, and these parties are work. You get invited if you have business to transact. Certain deals, Elizabeth has since told me, can only be made with a drink in your hand and a woman in a cocktail dress by your side. The Census doesn't work that way, but Defense, where Elizabeth works, does.

I arrived late because the woman who brought me wanted to know why I wouldn't sleep with her. I befriended her because her husband had died rushing to the hospital because their son put himself into a coma with cocaine; I thought she needed my help. "You don't know how gorgeous you are, do you?" she said when I told her thank you, but no.

"Don't joke," I said. I didn't believe her, though I've learned over the past year a half that I maybe should have respected her eye more. Elizabeth came up to me ten minutes after I arrived and asked me if I worked for Defense or State. "I'm on the domestic side," I told her.

And she told me, "Well, I've talked to all the people I need to here. Are you ready to go?"

I must have sniffed something about her, because I took a quick look back at my hostess, downing a highball glass she brimmed with scotch, and I said, "Lead on."

4.

Elizabeth was the first woman I slept with the first time I met her. She always said she felt an instinctual attraction between us. Me, I'm wary of instinct. Even the bees: when they mate, instinct draws all the drones, but only the fastest, strongest, most agile male succeeds. Of course, after he delivers sperm enough to last the queen a year or more, she heads back to the hive with his member still in her. What's left of him drops out of the air like a stone. So, instinct makes all the drones fly, but instinct doesn't always result in success. And even success seems no more than a limited success, taken from the individual drone's point of view. Maybe instinct drives the hive, maybe instinct drives society for us, but I find it hard to imagine what instinct means for the individual bee, or person.

But I have no other explanation for what happened that night. I didn't know where she led me, but I followed. A bar? Her place? In the two-block walk we talked about the party, or she talked about it. "No one has even a second for fun at these things," she told me. "You try to measure how fast you drink so that when you finally get the chance to talk to the power man you're there to see, you aren't too drunk to make sense or too sober to ask for what you want. And when you're done, always unsure whether you've made any real impact, you slap down another drink and head for the door. This is my car." She pointed at a sleek red Porsche.

She leaned her seat against the passenger door. I thought we'd hang there in the chilly fall night and discuss where to go next, but she took the lapels of my jacket and pulled me to her. Her mouth laid open, wide and wet, and I felt her tongue draw my front teeth closer into her. I had to support myself against the roof to stop myself from crushing her. Her hips rolled in a slow-motion dance against me. I think I remember her hand jockeying back and forth from stick-shift to me on the ride in her car, but I can only say for certain that half an hour after we left the party we were naked in her bed.

5.

I met Elizabeth's father only once before the crisis with Elizabeth. I don't want to tell you her last name, because you'd recognize it from the investment firm her family's been part of for a couple of generations. He's a big man who wears deep heavy dark suits that smell of old furniture. He comes across, in pictures, as an overstuffed chair. But in person he's always grunting and grumbling, roving and rumbling, no chair you'd settle into. Elizabeth says people who work with him know to pay attention only when he mumbles; that's when he really means what he says.

I don't mean to make her father out as an old cartoon

money sack, one of those drawstring numbers, with a dollar sign on the front, that always crushes the badly-shaven thief. He raises funds for research for the blind, supports art museums, and chairs international trade associations. When he comes to DC, he meets Elizabeth for a drink at his hotel or they end up at the same functions. He seemed to like me the one time he met me, though how he assayed my value as a potential son-in-law even Elizabeth couldn't say.

"No one can read my father, though he expects everyone to," she told me.

His resume tells more about Elizabeth's upbringing than about his personality. Elizabeth grew up in New York private schools, then went on to Choate, Brown and the Fletcher School, all the cream of education. She was twenty-three when she took her first job, with the Defense Department. She became an expert on the effects of defense spending on international economies, especially in the Middle East. I can't begin to hold in my head the number of variables she works with every day. She loves her work more than she loves anybody, and in five years has become the second-ranking civilian woman in the Department. I don't think she had to use her looks to rise so fast; she pays only offhand attention to her appearance anyway. She goes in for what she calls a general workup every two weeks—hair, facial, nails. In between, she thinks less about her skin, clothes and style than the average riveter. She smells of charm, kindness, money and as much honesty as her work allows.

When the bees want to raise a queen, either to swarm or to replace an old one, the nurse bees feed a regular fertilized worker-larva nothing but royal jelly. That's all it takes. Without royal jelly, they get a worker; with it they get a queen. So what makes people think we are so different?

6.

Elizabeth and I have a tacit arrangement: we stay out of each other's families. This means we won't marry, of course, but once I knew Elizabeth I guess I knew that. Moving in together three months after we first met and slept together just streamlined home life. Elizabeth doesn't like thinking about clothes, and splitting time between places meant she had to. She had already agreed to buy a big new place before we met. After she closed we both moved in, and I pay her rent. When I protested she wanted too little, she told me, "Don't be ridiculous. There's no way to calculate my tax benefit, and you don't have the sort of money I do." Then she wrinkled up her nose and put her lips into the narrow smile she gets before she laughs. "Anyway, I like having a man around the house. It keeps my juices flowing. I work better when I hear the grunts of a football game coming from the next room."

I took a second to realize she was teasing me. Football season was over a couple months already, so I knew she wasn't talking about television. But I used to play for Ohio State, ten years ago. I never started, except a few games my last two years when the real tight ends got busted or had busted something up. I played special teams, swarming under the ball after a kick. She tweaked my nose like that all the time. Often as not she was in the other room before I realized I'd been tweaked.

But football got me to college, which I could never have afforded otherwise. My dad worked the line at the plant when I was younger, and my mother worked half-time checkout at a supermarket in the north end, away from our home, my dad's plant and my schools. My dad wouldn't have liked her working, but if she wanted the two of us to eat she had no choice. Dad drank. Most of what he earned went into a cigar box under the bar of one of the taverns in the industrial part of town.

Seventh grade, before I grew so big, I came home on a January afternoon. The sky hung grey, ready for an early dark. When I got to our semi-detached, I knew something had gone wrong. My father's car angled across the drive-way and the front door cocked open, despite the cold. I ran into the house unzipping my coat. The second I opened my mouth to call out, my father bulled around the hall corner and smacked me with the back of his hand across my face. "I bet you knew all along, you skunk!" I slumped against the spindly table by the door. As I shook myself upright, his tires coughed up frozen ground and peeled his car down the street, through the stop sign at the corner and out of sight.

I found my mother in the hallway outside the bathroom, bloody and disheveled. I had looked for her first in the kitchen, and that's where I saw the chair broken to splinters and all the cleaning mixtures tossed from under the sink. The blood, thank God, had come only from her nose, when she got hit there by a box of detergent he hurled at her, in apparent rage at supermarket products. A guy on the line with Dad had just moved to the north end, and his wife had gotten into a conversation with Ma, and so the word got back about my mother's job. I helped Ma to the kitchen. While she washed herself in the sink, she kept saying, "Try to understand your father. I lied to him. He's never lied to me, not ever."

7.

That was the first time he hit either of us. Over the next few years our house became a circus of violence and apology. Every month or so, Dad rustled up another outburst. When he decided he would save money by staying out of bars and drinking at home, I started to get interested in sports.

It took my body a couple of years to cooperate with me, but by the time I was fifteen I'd grown to 5′9″. Lifting made each inch muscular. Dad mostly exploded at the house, the furniture, the dishes, but sometimes he went for Ma or me. As I grew bigger he stopped coming after me. Then, once, he just took it in his head to hurl his glass at my mother from his drinking chair. He caught her with the rim above the eye and she went down, bleeding and screaming. I charged up from the basement, where I was doing curls with the little weights Coach let me take home, and right away I knew what he'd done. Usually I go to Ma, help her, see what I can do to make someone better, rather than make the whole thing worse, but this time my adrenaline already pumped through me from lifting and I went right over to Dad.

I didn't touch him. I swear I didn't. I thought I was going to, and he thought so too. His eyes greyed like I was Judgment, and he froze. I put my face in his and tried to shout, but his fear plugged up my words. So close to him, I did what I could. I kissed him at his failing hairline and with my right hand I set his bottle on its side, so the vodka glugged out into his chair. Then I went to help Ma.

I think he wanted to hit me then, kick me, smash me with the bottle, scream, but he didn't. He just looked at the draining alcohol, just to stare off at something not me and not Ma.

He never hit either of us again, but the drinking didn't stop. We just accommodated him, as though his concession not to hit us should have rendered us so grateful we should accept his nightly stupor, his illnesses, his unpredictable kindnesses without question.

8.

My freshman year at college, my father moved into a white-collar job. Line Consultant, I think they called him. Though I went to school less than fifty miles from my home, I lived away, only in part because the team mostly lived and ate together. We played Thanksgiving, so Christmas break was my first time home. The house creaked with weariness much more than when I'd left. When my father came home that first night he seemed to be choked by the polyester tie around his throat.

My mother had told me how pleased and proud she was of Dad for getting into management, but Dad didn't share her enthusiasm. He said nothing as he lumbered through the kitchen to the bathroom, a whole fist yanking the knot of the tie from his neck, and only, "Welcome home, son," as he took the bottle and glasses from the cupboard on his way into the living room. "Join me in a drink later?" he said without looking at me, only tinkling the glasses to mark me as his audience.

"He talks a little more about stopping," Ma said.

"Has he cut down at all?"

"Oh, Lord, yes. I don't think he drinks before he gets home at all now. And I've been diluting the bottle little by little," she whispered, "to wean him."

An hour later, when I went in to talk with him, you couldn't tell Ma had diluted the bottle. His eyes couldn't decide between themselves what to focus on, so his right one chose me and the left some of the silk flowers my mother had taken up as a paying hobby. "I'm proud of you, Dad. New job!"

"Want a drink? Have a drink!"

"No, no thanks." He poured one anyway. I never drank at all in those days, took a sharp will around football players. "So tell me about the job."

"You know why they gave me this job?"

"Twenty years on the line seems good enough to me."

"That's because you don't know the line. They'll keep you there long as you can do the job."

"So why'd they move you?"

"Because I blacked out."

"That can happen to anyone, happens at least once a week at practice."

"I didn't faint or nothing. I mean I blacked out. Standing there doing my job and I don't know where I am or what I'm doing. It'd been happening for years, but I just figured it comes with knowing the job so well. The boss didn't see it that way."

I eyed him close, because I'd learned that he got thirstier when he hid some gravel in his gullet, and often as not you could see him studying how to spit the gravel out. "Did someone get hurt, Dad?"

He shook his head hard. "Not bad, anyway. They tell me I shot a few staples across the room, but no one got hit. I can't say, I can't say."

"So they gave you an office off the line."

He nodded. "The doc said I have to stop drinking. The boss says if I don't do what the doc says they'll have to can me. Son, I can't do it, I just can't."

I had never seen my father cry before, and I didn't want to see him cry now. I went out to find some friends. When

I came home, my mother sat working on her flowers at the kitchen table and my father slept half-dressed on their bed. I noticed the living room couch neatly made up, too, and it took no brains to realize Ma had been sleeping in my room since I'd gone away.

9.

So perhaps with different parents I would have responded to Elizabeth's phone message with a message of my own. My mother didn't like the life her husband made for her, and my father didn't ask for alcoholism. Don't think I didn't know how rare a chance Ohio State made for me, but I couldn't have made one for myself any more than they could have. Perhaps I was that one bee who could find the relocated hive, could see football and college as an opportunity a little diligence could earn me. But I didn't choose to grow big, and I only chose to get strong when my survival depended on it. Bees become what they eat. People too, but people eat the lives their families lead.

Of course, a bee can't survive without the hive but people can. Once we leave home we can make something new of ourselves. Take Jim. He grew up in Dee-troit, as he calls it, city-boy to the bone, but now he's working with some Virginia truck farmers, friends of some third cousins who live in DC. They've got nearly a thousand acres in cultivation all over Rockland County, and Jim handles all the organically grown produce, about three hundred acres he bought close in to the city. He eats conscientiously and meditates: a strapping black man from Murder Central, part of the sprouts-for-lunch bunch. A real self-made man, the way I look at it.

We met in a game my sophomore year at Ohio State, his freshman at Michigan. Opening kickoff, he received, the new college phenom. Ten steps later, I planted him like a corpse. It felt like a rock when we both landed square on the ball. The refs gave it to Jim's Wolverines, though neither of us had a cell of skin on it. He twitched a bit as he got up and yelled at me, "G-g-g-g-g-good hit, f-f-f-fucker!" Then he jogged awkwardly off the field.

The rest of the game I'm worrying about him. Damn, did I hit him too hard? He looked so spastic, so shaky. And that stutter! Maybe he won't tell his coach how he feels. Maybe they play their guys hurt. Maybe his brain's bleeding, for God's sake! Damn. The rest of the game I'm watching him like a mother. He totes up the yards, but he's running all jangly. He screws up, then he screws us. I'm the one missing tackles, missing signals, because I worry I damaged this guy.

So after the game I run across the field. So does everyone else, that sportsman-handshake rag, but I want to find Jim, see he's all right. I can't find him. A hundred guys in uniform, how am I supposed to?

I stop a teammate of his, a guy mumbling, "Good game, good game," to anyone wearing my colors.

"Yeah, you too. Have you seen Jim Polder?"

This guy gets a devilish light in his eye. "J-j-j-j-jim? The star of the g-g-g-game? He's talking to T-T-T-TV!" He cracks up and runs toward the locker room. I put my fanny down on their bench and feel like an utter dope.

10.

We stayed friends afterwards. He went into pro ball, because he could. I finished college, took the civil service exam and applied for jobs away from Ohio. Jim came to the Redskins the year I got promoted out of data entry at the Bureau. He started keeping bees over at his place, outside of town, and when he went away asked me to look in on them, make sure there was water in the nearby birdbath and so on. "I don't want nothing untoward to happen," he told me.

I go out for a look, a cloudy squally kind of day, waltz over to the entrance and bend over to peek in. A dozen of them came after me at once. One stung my nose and another got my forehead. Half a squeal later, I was inside and what looked to me like the rest of the hive battered themselves against the screen door coming after me.

I watched them for a while from there, and then picked through Jim's library for books on bees and beekeeping. "Never approach the entrance to a beehive. That is sufficient provocation for most guard bees." Aha! "Inclement weather makes bees temperamental." Aha again! I spent the whole day there reading, took a handful of books with me and stopped at the library on my way home for even more. The creatures hooked me then and there. While I read, I nursed the throbbing bumps on my face, easing the swelling with ice wrapped in paper towel. Three hundred bee stings will kill the average man, but two will teach him a lesson good enough to last his whole life.

11.

We have ten hives in a copse at the middle of Jim's contiguous farms and another couple in the middle of each of the orchards; the apple blossom and cherry blossom honeys sell very well. But the stand of trees is where we go on these evening visits, especially when the weather is fine, as it has been all spring. Winters, Jim builds around his place. He put up a swinging bench, two Adirondack chairs and a tire at the northern edge of the copse. The bees buzz around on their way to the bean and pea fields up that way. We came out without the netting, a spring survey of coming work. Once the farms kick into production, Jim doesn't have time for the bees anymore. They're mine anyway; we keep them out here because Jim needs their help growing food.

"So how's Queen Elizabeth?" Jim's stutter has faded as he's grown older. He's also gotten thinner since he gave up meat, weight-lifting and beer with the boys. The jangle in his walk is now a dancer's stride. All that bulk made him awkward in his own skin.

"Fine. Off to Newport for some meeting."

"When did she t-t-tell you?" When the words still catch, Jim bangs the tips of his long left-hand fingers against his thigh. Most of his work pants have a worn patch at the bottom of that front pocket. The light tap "gets my record spinning," says Jim.

"Found a message when I got home."

"Any other woman, I'd swear she was stepping out on you."

"Elizabeth?"

"D-d-don't lay on me it hasn't run cross your mind."

"Sure. Not much I can do about it though, is there?"

"Not with that attitude."

"What attitude?"

"You know. You t-t-told me sitting here a year ago, and you told me again this fall. 'She's out of my league. I'm lucky she lets me stay in the game.'"

"True words. I'd say them again."

"If you were playing football, I'd say you're right: one game with the big boys and you get a desk job for life." Jim always teases me about my work. "People in love don't have leagues that way."

"Wisdom from the expert!" Jim had such high romantic ideals he could never have a romance. He'd survived on temporary liaisons with organically-minded college kids who came to work the farm with him most summers. I teased him about love the way he got on me about work. "Big words from the big lover!"

Jim laughs his hacking chuckle. "Don't fool yourself. Those girls put themselves to sleep thinking about how big."

I say, "Elizabeth loves her work. At least she calls when she won't be coming home."

"You don't have nothing to worry about with her and other lovers, not for a while. That woman is married to her work." Jim had met Elizabeth half a dozen times, mostly at parties I'd dragged her to. But I had learned to trust Jim's intuition about people, and he'd learned more about her when she'd come out for dinner that first winter than I had in the two months we'd known each other. Jim somehow coaxed Elizabeth out. All I had seen of her had been either work-mode or sex. Not that we never talked, just that she related to me woman to man instead of person to person. I don't say I minded.

But with Jim she relaxed. We drank two bottles of wine, the three of us, and talked about bees. The only bit of conversation I remember, we told her about supercedure. When a hive senses that the queen has run low on sperm—

some queens get enough on their one nuptial flight to last six or seven years, but one or two years is more typical— the worker bees plot to overthrow her. Some say she loses a certain smell, others that the workers notice an increase in drone, or unfertilized, larvae. In any case, they build big queen cells into the honeycomb, several of them up near the top where the queen rests, and over the course of a couple of weeks they raise a crop of princesses. The first one out often tries to kill the others, but the workers guard their cache of royalty. If the princess survives to a successful nuptial flight, the two queens fight. If the old queen wins, the workers release another princess; if she loses, as she usually does, the workers help the new queen kill the other princesses, the potential threats in their cells.

"Of course," Jim told Elizabeth, "sometimes the hive just turns on the queen. Too much r-r-rough handling, or heat, or water and the hive blames the queen. Before you know it, the workers flock around her. The have little hooks on their feet they latch together, thousands of them. And then they squeeze. And squeeze. And squeeze."

I said, "We call it 'balling the queen.' "

Elizabeth looked at me the way she does, like the room's too light and there are too many people, and said, "I thought that's what the drones did."

Later we went out in the cold dark of the country and walked around the hives. They were mostly single or double-levels then, and quiet as a pantry. After we stood in the cold watching the pale and silent boxes, she said, "They make better stories than they do company, don't they?" Alone, I never feel that people are smarter than bees. Elizabeth always makes me feel that some of us are.

"She's a working girl, down to her bones," Jim was saying. "She's married to her employment. That's why she never treats you like a mate. She already has one. That's why she won't have someone else. You're already her p-p-piece on the side. C'mon and see the Control Tower."

We named one hive the Control Tower because we had stacked eight supers and the hive seemed overjoyed to just keep growing. Healthy hives go about sixty or eighty thousand, and we figure this one up about one-fifty, maybe more. It all started that night with Elizabeth. I noticed what looked like the start of swarm cells down below, very strange for winter.

This hive had an especially fertile queen for a year, and we'd put on two more frames for them in the summer. But now that wasn't enough room and they had thoughts of dividing. Then a freak storm terrified another hive into assassination, not a good queen to start with, and a very discontented hive. So Jim and I stacked that hive onto the Control Tower and separated them with some newspaper covered with sugar water. The bees ate through the paper, and the strong hive below started a program of eugenics, killing off the bees who met the standards of the old queen but wouldn't make it in their new home. By now, the queen was two-and-half and going strong laying worker brood.

"Oh, man, look at this mess!" Every time the bees showed a hint of swarming, like the last time I was out, we quieted them down with another super of empty frames. Of course, we'd destroy their swarm cells too, the queen cells they build at the bottom of the hive, to raise a new queen who will lead half the hive to a new home. More room calmed the Control Tower, but every time we stacked another frame, the bees would seal the joints with propolis. Normally, with any other hive, we'd crowbar free any combs or frames or supers linked with this sticky cement, because you couldn't get the honey any other way. But with the Control Tower we'd given up the idea of honey. We were shooting for the stars. We're climbing up super by super. I said, "You think Elizabeth is married to her work, take a look at these guys."

"They got to have some phenomenal birth and survival rate. I think maybe they got a second queen in there."

"So what am I supposed to do about Elizabeth?"

"I dunno. What are you supposed to do about these b-b-bees?"

I made him a face he knew. I don't joke with anybody they way I joke with Jim, but sometimes he knows I don't want to joke even with him.

"OK, OK," he conceded. But then he asked, "If you were her fancy man, what would you do?"

"Depends."

"On what?"

"On whether I wanted more from her. On if she made me jealous. On if I thought I could have some other kind of relationship with her."

"What do you want now?"

"Nothing. I like it how it is."

"Dude?"

"I get to be around her. We sleep together every night—"

"Uh-huh."

"—almost every night. She tells me I help her work. I don't know how; I don't understand ninety-five percent of what she does. But she says I help her, and that's enough for me right now."

"And when you want to hitch?" Jim gets down on his hands and knees to check the bottom of the hive for swarm cells. "Nothing down there but some cleaning bees, old ones. Amazing." Usually young bees cleaned and old bees died, but in the Control Tower the young bees cleaned the cells and the old bees, whose ragged wings kept them from foraging now, worked at sweeping away the tremendous accumulation at the bottom of so large a hive.

I get down on the other side to look. "Sure is." I sat back on my heels listening to the din of this huge city. "I'm only thirty-two. Am I in a hurry to marry?"

"Would you marry Queen Elizabeth?"

"Maybe for the money." We laughed, but then I said, "I could never keep her, so why try?"

"So why stay?"

I stand and cross over to inspect the other hives: The Embassy, Department of the Treasury, Langley. We named most of them for their similarity in character to DC landmarks. "I'm never going to get it this good again."

"Or this b-b-bad," Jim corrects me.

"Or this bad," I admitted.

12.

Elizabeth came home late the next night, Thursday. Fall and spring I play softball Thursday nights and so over the months we assigned no plans to that night. We don't call each other—which is to say I don't call her—during the day to set dinner. We never count on that night together. So we didn't talk, even though my spring league hadn't begun yet. I scrounged a meal from the restaurant take-out containers in the fridge and began reading *Census Monthly, Population Reports* and the other trade journals. Diligence doesn't end at the Bureau doors.

I heard her key before I heard her. "Ron?" she called. She walked past my study door, where I sat with my feet up and a reading light on. She had a shopping bag in her hand and her suit on. She'll shed that suit first chance she gets, so I knew for sure she'd been working late.

"Here!" I didn't get up.

"Ron?" This time she turned into the study. I could see from her walk how tired she was; she shuffled like an exhausted child when she needed sleep. In one motion, she knelt and laid her head on my chest, mumbling there, "Hi, honey."

Her hair glistened red and brown, like a chestnut polished for a Christmas display. I kissed it. "Hi. Rough day?"

She wriggled up and nibbled my shoulder, my cheek, my moustache, my lips. She sat back on her heels. "Two rough days." She shrugged off her coat. "Yesterday started out of control, when that report I'd worked on last week, the Greece-Turkey one, came out of the computer printed like a chart." She twisted sideways and unzipped her skirt, breathed deep as she loosed the top button. She slid her shoes off her heels behind her, then brought her legs up and rested her chin on her knees.

"Have I told you how sexy you are?" she said, smiling. "That was when the General called. 'Got a special project hatching, Elizabeth. I think we could use your help with.' He always talks to me like a high school guidance counselor, I don't know why." She lifted her hips and pulled the hem of her skirt and slip. She kicked them off with one foot and then giggled at me. That's how she gave away she knew this was a show and I was the audience. I'd never call on her to cut it out. She liked undressing in front of me, and I loved it. I always watched, and I always knew she'd be hurt if I didn't. I threw her a kiss.

She leaned over, head to knees, stretching. Her toes pointed, her hair waves of color on the deep-blue Persian. By the time she sat back up, she'd unbuttoned her blouse, which fell open around the lace-flowered cups of her bra. She leaned back on her hands, swaying side to side as she talked, almost cheap, airing herself like that, but still a rich indulgence for me.

"So I rush over to his office, trying to think what he wants me for. Usually when he calls it's for statistics on this or a quick answer to that. You know he thanks me for my reports but doesn't read them. Other people do, colonels and so on. They never listen to recommendations from civilians anyway. A civilian woman?" She turned sultry for that one word, and then snapped herself right back, I never knew how she handled herself so well. Then she mimicked a martial voice and said, "Never let your pride slip so low, men. Never let the military down."

She shrugged the straps of her bra off her shoulders and bent her left leg to release her stocking from her garter. This part I love. She knows it too.

"It turns out that enough people credited my ideas on Israel and Egypt and the Emirates that he wanted to talk to me personally, to see if I could handle more than words and paper. 'Well, Elizabeth' "—she hesitated, hooded her eyes and began massaging the inside of her thighs; I felt myself giving up to her totally, enthralled, but too dazzled by the show to want to stop it—" 'Elizabeth, we've got a new trouble-spot for you. It's a bit bigger, a bit more complicated. Feel like getting away from your books for a while?' Of course I did. 'Gooooood! We fly to Newport after lunch. Big meetings tomorrow. It's ten-fifteen now. Close up all your other business and meet me here at thirteen hundred. We'll be gone overnight.' " She peeled down both stockings and threw them at me. Her legs look smoother bare than covered, translucent and muscular. I love Elizabeth's legs, I love her whole body, so small and lean and perfumed like soil and flowers.

"I knew he meant tie it all up and so I did, as best I could. By the time I got back to him the plans had changed. We met all afternoon with people from State and then we conference-called with the White House." She looked tickled. "I've never been this high before," she said. Looking at her, feeling as I felt, she could have meant anything, but I knew what she meant. She meant the power pyramid. She felt dizzy from the climb. She always stood where the air thinned out to less than I could breathe.

"Then later, on board the plane, the General ran down the people we'd meet in Newport, big brass from Navy mostly, and a professor I'd met at a conference during grad school. We met until midnight and began again this morning. I came home right from the airfield." She unsnapped the front of her bra, and it trickled off behind her. Her breasts, so soft and freckled, so alive, called me. My journals fell as I rose from my chair and I picked Elizabeth up. I could hardly catch my breath, but still, she was so light she didn't even need to support herself with her arms around my neck. She dropped her head back and laughed and laughed as I carried her to the bedroom.

13.

A hour or more passed before I caught my breath again. "Ron?" she whispered after a silence that felt like sleep.
"Yeah?"
"It's Lebanon."
"What's Lebanon?"
"That's what I spent the past couple of days working on. That's what I'm going to be spending the next several months working on."
"Is that bad?"
"It could be."
"Why?"
"It's dangerous."
"Only if you go there. Will you have to?"
"I might. I don't know."
"So?"

"It's not only me, you know. I'm in charge of research on this. I'm in the planning group. If I screw up, someone can get hurt."

I didn't say anything. I felt out of my depth, like I did whenever Elizabeth talked about her work. But she never asked for my help in work, except when sometimes she needed to know population and housing and other numbers. I know the facts, I just don't know what they mean. "You don't order anybody to do anything. It's not your fault if they get hurt."

"Maybe."

"Yeah, maybe."

She said, "I shouldn't even tell you this. It's classified."

"But?"

"I need to tell someone. You don't know anyone this will matter to and it helps me to say 'I'm scared' out loud."

"Go ahead."

"I'm scared!" she said full voice, and then let loose a jittery chuckle. "Thank you, Ron."

"You never have to thank me."

"I know, I know: faithful servant." I sometimes sign my notes to her that way. I'm a civil servant and she's not. "But thank you anyway."

"One thing, though. I do know someone this will matter to."

She stiffened. "Who?"

"Me. You can tell me anything you want."

I don't remember if we said anything else. Sooner than I would have believed morning came with the radio-alarm and a day of rules and averages and distractions. Friday could not have come at a better time.

14.

That spring showed us the most perfect weather Washington's drained swamp ever has. Day after day, the sun bristled with proud accomplishment as it shone on the blooming earth. Flowers outdid themselves in quiet fireworks. The mall thronged with international tourists, agog with the magnificence of our capital. The city shimmered in excitement.

Elizabeth never explained Defense's intentions in Lebanon to me, but she never stopped describing the place. I read the paper during my morning break now, instead of sticking to my reports and categories. "Dateline: Beirut" yanked my attention from the sports and funnies; I just wanted to do what I could to support Elizabeth, who had never tried talking so much to me about her actual work. In the past, she'd told me about the people in her department. "You're the expert on people," she would say. "I'm the expert on the world."

I wouldn't say I'm an expert on people. I don't even work in the population section of the Bureau. Housing Characteristics, where I work, defines living alternatives: who lives with whom and in what. I think that tells a host about people, but only taken as a group. I don't think I know much more about an individual psyche than most anyone. Especially not Elizabeth.

But the weather and Elizabeth's newfound talkativeness bred an expansiveness in our lives. Work became even more important for Elizabeth than it had before, it's true, but during those few hours she leaned away from her desk she wanted to be out in the world. We ate out together, and she even came out to the country a couple of times, to 'help' me and Jim handle the Control Tower. She mostly just sat in one of the Adirondack chairs, gazing into the fields, far more beautiful and stylish than you see in fashion ads bent on staging an event like that. Elizabeth could be composed if she were the only ex-girlfriend at a jilted boyfriend's wedding. Beaming in the spring sun, legs strained against her blue-jean pedal pushers, surrounded by an oversized cowl-necked sweatshirt, green like her eyes, Elizabeth acted like she knew how to accept the buzz of a thousand bees around her.

15.

I came home one day and found Elizabeth huddling under a comforter on the couch. Her hair turned dark sticking to her wet temples. I couldn't tell her sweat from her tears, but I almost enjoyed the rare pleasure of coming home to her. She had gone to New York for a meeting with a trade association, heavy-hitting businessmen with connections all over the Middle East. Her father sat on the group's board, on and off. So he was there, might have wrangled the invitation for Elizabeth to talk to them. She had expected a lot from the speech, but she seemed to have gotten more than she could handle.

I soothed her. "What's wrong?"

"He doesn't know how much he upsets me when he does that."

"He was just helping you out. Just talking you up."

"He wasn't, he wasn't. He just couldn't stop being my father."

"He is your father. Why should he stop?"

"You don't get it, Ron. You just don't."

"So explain it to me." I never have trouble believing I'm not getting it. "Tell me what happened."

"It's a breakfast meeting. I'm the only woman in the room, the only person under thirty, maybe under forty, and he tells everyone in the room that I'm the image of my mother."

"Tell them how? Not a speech?"

"Just in conversation."

"He's proud. He's proud of you."

"You don't know my father. Everyone in the room knows what happened to my mother, so later, when it's time for my presentation, they're looking for signs. I scan the room and everyone's studying me like I have TRAGEDY written on my forehead. They're not hearing a word I say." She kicked the sofa arm hard with her bare heel. "You think he doesn't know, but he does. He knows exactly what he's doing."

She coughed a sob and then another. I'm still in my suitcoat and tie, perched on the edge of the couch. "It's all right," I soothed, "your father still loves you."

She couldn't push out the words at first, but after a shallow gasp she hoarsed, "Not like I am!" Then her face disintegrated, bits going every way. I folded her in my arms in the comforter and rocked her and rocked her. I didn't think she'd ever stop crying.

16.

I learned that Lebanon had once been a country. Reading the news reports, you might think it still is, just one where the rules we think of as governing countries had taken a temporary holiday. Elizabeth says that's not true. "One of the reasons," she wrote in a report she let me read, "political scientists follow Lebanon so closely is that countries rarely fall so precipitously from power to brigandage.

"Lebanon had been a center for trade in the Middle East right into the 1970's. Compared to its neighbors, Lebanon displayed a cosmopolitan acceptance of cultural difference, a sophistication only tolerance can prove.

"Of course, nothing in the land which used to go by the name Lebanon looks like a country any more. Even Beirut, which had been a gem of international trade not two decades ago, now looks as though adolescents with modern weaponry took a field trip there. The city has lost all hope of resurrection, and the country of which it remains the titular capital has become the possession of the various private armies. The closest parallel in European history is the Italy of the Condotterei, who began as contract enforcers and learned in time they did not need a contract with local authority to take what they wanted.

"This condition leaves the territory—which is how we must refer to the land—peculiarly vulnerable to . . . ."

Elizabeth's report never made clear to me what she meant about Lebanon's vulnerability. All I could see, when I read the articles in the paper, were people fighting each other over religion, the Christians and the Muslims banging each other into the ground. I didn't need Elizabeth's kind of education to know that had been happening since the Crusades. Growing up in the Midwest you see all the squabbling over religion you have a taste for. And if the Christians there don't have anyone else to attack, they'll just choose sides among themselves.

17.

Late one early May afternoon, my father showed up at my office.

He did not make an impressive entrance to my department. I had been working in Housing Characteristics for more than five years by then, and had gotten a promotion into my own office three years before, ahead of some people who had been there longer. I did have a college degree and I took some night courses in advanced statistics and information management, so my promotion had not come out of favoritism, or prejudice, or—as I heard a whisper once—because football players always intimidated people. But that didn't make it easier for people to accept me, and I had worked hard, still worked hard, at making people in the office like me. I felt very exposed, windowed in that office by myself, but still on view for my co-workers' censure.

He appeared on a day when Virginia, my secretary, stayed home with her kids. She always had some trouble because one of the kids was deaf and the other was retarded and she wasn't married—a black single woman head of household, as the people in Population characterized her. She needed a lot of time off. So instead of Virginia, Bea, one of the people who handled requests for information from inside the government, had been there for decades, came knocking on my open door.

"Mr. Stutzer, there's a man outside here says he wants to see you."

"OK," I said getting up, "thank you." Bea had called me Ron when we worked side by side, but for three years now she's called me Mr. Stutzer and I can't change her.

"But Mr. Stutzer, I don't think he's safe."

"What do you mean, not safe?"

"He's been drinking!" Her eyes widened to the size of the flowers on her print dress. Bea joined the Jehovah's Witnesses the year before to help her break a problem she had with pills, and she let anyone who mentioned drink know what she now thought of it.

My heart went hard in my chest. "Did he say what he wants?"

"He said he wants to see his son."

I told her, "We all have our crosses, Bea. My father's mine."

"If you don't mind my saying it, he looks like he slept in his clothes," she confided as I walked past her out my office door. "Do you think the Witnesses might help?"

I took two cups of coffee from the alcove machine and steered my father out to the elevators. He looked like he had slept not one but several nights in his clothes, and in bus stations to boot. I dreaded the talk Bea would spread around my people once we left, but if I had to talk with him, I wanted him out in the air. Didn't the security people have any sense of smell?

"Dad, what are you doing here?"

"I came for the cherry blossoms, but I guess I'm a little late."

"Where's Ma?"

"She's back at the ranch."

"A hotel?"

"Why would she stay in a hotel? The house not good enough for her?"

"So she's still back in Ohio."

"Your office doesn't look much different from mine."

"An office is an office. What are you doing in Washington?"

"I told you: I came for the cherry blossoms, but they wouldn't wait. Didn't want to die without seeing the capital in bloom."

I could see his eyes hardly focused at all, worse than I remembered seeing him for a long time. I couldn't bring him home, I knew that. I didn't want to. But I had to help him. "How are you fixed for money, Dad? You got a place to stay?"

"Never much trouble finding a place, if you know where to look. I thought I'd stay with you for a while."

"No can do. The place is too small, and I already have somebody staying there."

"A girl?"

"No. Jim, Jim Polder. My football friend."

"The nigger?"

"Let me find you a hotel this afternoon." I took out my wallet and handed him the $60 I had there. "Meet me in the park there, across the street, between six-thirty and seven. And we'll get you fixed up. Do you have a suitcase somewhere?" He stared at the bills in his hand and started crying then, tears dropping onto the money and pooling there. "Dad?" I said. "Dad?"

"I had a suitcase, but I can't remember where I left it."

"Dad? Are you listening? Dad? Take that money, buy yourself some clothes, some toiletries. Here, take my credit card, charge what you need. Meet me here at six-thirty, that's two and a half hours. In the park across the street. You understand?" He squinted at the credit card in his hand, which was as smudged and ragged as it had been his days on the line. "Dad, do you understand me?"

He looked at me, focused for a second and nodded. "I understand."

"Six-thirty. At the park." I went back inside and began calling hotels.

18.

"The C-c-control Tower has gone out of control," Jim's message said that evening. "They turned out to be nothing but thieves."

The fountain and the pigeons were the only movement in the park near my office when I left at seven-thirty. I had no idea what had become of Dad. Could he have found out where I lived and gone there? Checked into a hotel? Cleared a liquor store shelf and reduced himself to a stupor? I pretended to read, perched on the edge of the fountain, while I really checked the time, the streets, my imagination for what had become of him.

I had no place else to go but home. Elizabeth's project built up in intensity those first weeks in May, and her occasional trips out of town never took her away overnight. Even those nights we dined together, she'd work into morning hours; in some way I relished missing dinner with her because then she'd get to bed early enough for me to soothe her, massage her back and thighs, stroke her head, pamper her.

The machine message signal flashed in the bedroom corner where we kept it. As I toyed with the buttons I could almost hear my father telling me he was fine, found a nice room in a nice hotel, sobered up. First came Jim, though, and then Elizabeth, saying she'd be home by ten, and then nothing, just the hollow hiss of overused and inexpensive tape.

I called Ohio. "Ma, it's Ron. Where's Dad?"

"Oh, Ron, how are you, love?"

"I'm fine."

"I worry sometimes I don't hear from you weeks on end."

"It's been a busy time, Ma. Where's Dad?"

"I don't know, I stopped trying to keep track of him."

"When was the last time you saw him?"

"Why the sudden interest in your father? You don't want to know how I'm doing?"

"I saw him today, Ma."

"Who?"

"Dad. Your husband."

"Saw him where? How?"

"Here, in Washington. He appeared at my office this afternoon. He looked like he was on day three of a weeklong tear. I gave him some money and found him a hotel room and now he's disappeared."

"He does that, you know. You can't let it get to you."

"I don't know where he is, Ma. No one knows where he is. I bet he doesn't even know where he is."

"What do you want me to do about it?"

"Did something happen, between you I mean?"

"Ron, it's just the same."

"What about his job?"

"If he's in Washington I guess he isn't working. I don't know."

The whole conversation seemed to be about a movie we saw the week before: interesting, but of no consequence. I stared at the sleek black phone machine—Elizabeth's, of course: high-tech and style together would be extravagance for me—until I felt like the machine was a communications black hole. Information went in, but nothing came out. My mother and I spoke across dimensions.

She said, "Ron, you all right?"

"Should I call the police, Ma? Should I?"

"Won't do much good. He's drunk in a heap somewhere or back on the road. Maybe he'll be back here tomorrow."

"I shouldn't do anything?"

"What can you do, Ron? It's in God's hands. Only Christ can save him, Ron, you know that."

Time to go.

"Yeah, Ma, OK. Call me if you hear from him, will you please?"

I freed myself from the phone and called Jim. He said Saturday would be soon enough, could Elizabeth come? That got us out there that day.

19.

"Elizabeth, you've g-g-got to see this!" Jim called, thwacking his thigh to release the stuck consonant.

"Where are they putting it all?" I wondered aloud to Jim. My eyes danced watching Elizabeth bound over from her Adirondack.

"They have so much room in there." We stood together and stared up and down the stacked supers weighted with frames full of honey.

"Look at the bees?" Elizabeth asked. "Look at you guys! Big macho football players nosing around in beehives."

"I wouldn't put your nose in that hive. I think these bees would take that too."

"What am I supposed to see?" Elizabeth stood as close to me as she could. Despite her cool around them, she never felt comfortable with the bees. She learned so fast about them I never needed to tell her twice to avoid the entrance to the hive, to stand still when around them, to keep her hair tied back so they wouldn't be tempted to burrow into it.

"Do you see that bee on the corner of the landing board?"

"The one talking to the others?"

I could see what she meant. The bee I meant busied herself unloading her pilfered honey to the nectar bees. "Yeah, but she's not talking. She's passing off goods."

"Don't they do that whenever they come in from the fields?"

"Uh-huh, but this is different. She's got honey there, not nectar."

"She stole it," Jim said.

"Where from?"

Jim pointed across the copse to Langley, a small hive named because they constantly intrigued, mostly against their queens, replacing even healthy, laying ones. They already had supercedure cells built as a threat against the queen they had raised just six weeks before. "She just went over there, pushed her way p-p-past one of the guards, sucked up a bellyful of honey and came home."

"So?"

"Bees don't do that," I told her.

"Looks like some bees do." Her eyes teased me.

"That's the point. Watch what she does next."

A couple of the guard bees came over to the thief and she touched antennas with them and then began to crawl up the side of the hive which faced Langley. She came back to the landing board and then flew a few fast tight circles around the hive. Some of the older bees came out of the hive, talked to her again, and again she flew around the hive and climbed the side facing Langley. Soon a group of bees were doing the same thing. Then they came back to the landing board for a frenzied huddle.

"Just like the locker room before the game," Jim whistled.

More bees piled on. There looked to be a couple of hundred. "They're going to ransack the place."

"What are you guys talking about?"

"You saw what that bee did?"

"Fly around, crawl around, touch antennas. Sure."

"She just told them where she found that honey and they're getting ready to go on a raid."

"All of them?"

A couple hundred bees buzzed in an excited mass by the landing board. I pointed to the fuzzy brown ball. "Most of those guys. A lot of guard bees, the bigger, stronger ones. Yup."

"Bees don't steal, Lizzie," Jim explained. "They collect nectar, they process it, they f-f-fan the nectar to evaporate the liquid and turn it into honey. But the Control Tower has gone from industry to indiscretion."

"They still do collect nectar," I added, "but it's a big hive. Some of them would rather just take the honey other hives make."

"They're taking off!" Elizabeth cried, and she leaned against me.

They charged straight for Langley, most of them. Langley guards sent out a warning, and the spooks inside dropped their plots against their queen and flew to the hive entrance.

Bees don't fight in uneven odds, usually, so most of the bees just fluttered around frantically while the guards battled one-on-one against the invaders. If a guard dropped, wings torn, abdomen punctured, sometimes another worker would take her place. But often as not the victor bee sucked up what honey it could and took off for home. One defender stung a departing thief and they both fell to the ground, but for the most part, the Control Tower won and Langley let them. Better than three-quarters of the strike force returned home with Langley's ready-made riches in their sacs.

"They been doing that two weeks so far, that I've noticed," Jim told me when it was over.

"Enough to ruin any other hive?"

"No, they're all strong this year. Langley's the weakest,

what with their new queens all the time. But I think the Tower just likes to show some muscle, now and again."

"Maybe there's something screwy with one of the supers or one of the frames. Maybe it just too tall for them to evaporate it right."

Elizabeth interrupted. "So these bees raid the others? What's the problem with it?"

Jim explained, "Usually bees only rob the weak. After a few raids, the weak hive gets discouraged, kills the queen, stops c-c-caring for brood. Can be trouble."

"But that's not happening."

"No, they take only a little each time, not enough to really hurt the other hive. Looks more like these bees are just out for a joy ride."

"Of course, that means we lose the honey they take, unless we decide to harvest the Control Tower."

Jim and I looked at each other and then at the tall, slender obelisk of life in front of us. Neither of us wanted to disturb the Tower, either the building or the bees inside, but we couldn't figure out what to do.

Elizabeth said, "Maybe the bees want you to harvest some honey, and that's what the raids are trying to say. They're big enough to destroy the other hives, right? So they must have some purpose in not doing it. Maybe they want *you* to raid *them*."

Jim laughed and nodded at me. "What do you say, pal?"

"When she's right," I put my hand on his shoulder, "she's right."

"Let's go get the ladder and tools."

"And nets. I'd rather be covered if Elizabeth is wrong."

20.

On the drive home in the lengthening, lingering evening, Elizabeth said to me, "It's begun. The Lebanon
thing."

"What do you mean?"

"What I've been working on. We set it in motion this
weekend."

"Shouldn't you be at work then? Should I drop you
off?"

She shook her head and watched the pale light coming
toward us through the dusk. "There's nothing I can do
now but wait"—she sighed—"and hope that I was right."

21.

Looking back, I can see how my life spun out of control
that week. I didn't notice while I lived it, though, sort of
like driving a big car around a tight curve: you lose control
of the vehicle well before your tires squeal. A mass of
metal hurtling along pavement at sixty miles an hour will
kill anything in its path, and most people know that, so the
moment those G-forces start to build we correct ourselves.

Most people survive highways, but life? What forces
build to tell you trouble's ahead? Forgetting appointments,
locking keys in a car, leaving mail unopened? You sure?
Then most people live life out of control.

During the week, I scoured the paper every day, hunting

up tidbits about Lebanon. I wanted to know what Elizabeth had worked on, and starting Monday of that week I hardly saw her. She flew to New York Wednesday, called Thursday, came home Friday, but the papers said nothing about her, about her work, about the Middle East even. I thought for a moment she'd lied to me, that the youth uprising in Jakarta had something to do with her, but I laughed away the thought. Not that she's beyond lying, particularly about her work. But Elizabeth is beyond a student demonstration gone wild with rocks and bottles and sticks, like what happened in Indonesia. She thinks bigger than that.

Later I realized that two short notices played a part in her complex scheme. One division of the Sixth Fleet began maneuvers South of Cyprus, "in preparation for any further breakdown between the governing parties on the island." And wildcat strikes slowed shipping in Tyre. If I had been Elizabeth and she me, she would have added something together from those notices. But I kept hunting for "Dateline: Beirut," and it never showed. My head buried itself in newspapers hours each day and came up at sunset empty.

The pit of my stomach felt empty too, wondering what had happened to my father. No use talking to Ma, she seemed gone about him. But he went beyond just seeming gone. Dad had disappeared. As quickly as he had shown he vanished, and I had nowhere to turn. A hero would have taken to the streets to look for him. Me, I called the police.

"Have you tried the homeless shelters?"

"He's not homeless. He has a very nice home in Cleveland."

"Cleveland Park?" That's a ritzy district of DC.

"No, Ohio."

"So why are you calling us?"

"Because last time I saw him he was here."

"In DC?"

"Yes. Have you picked up someone named Stutzer for drunkenness or vagrancy? That's all I want to know."

He grumbled something. "Hold on." The telephone gave that familiar click into blackness, and I stared out my office window for close to twenty minutes before a different voice came on the line.

The voice gave no salutation, just words like from a procedures manual. "We don't book drunks and vagrants. They go into a holding tank overnight, and in the morning we let them go. Each precinct has a tank, they take down their names, but they don't go onto a computer." I didn't answer. He hadn't asked a question. "You the one looking for the drunk, ain't you?" he asked.

"Yeah."

"Well, you got a question? I can put in a request, you should have information in a week. Or you can call each of the precincts and talk to the night clerk there. Eleven to seven. They know. Won't tell you where the man is, just if we'd seen him."

"How many precincts are there?"

"Lots. Listen, have you tried the homeless shelters?"

My heart also felt empty. You might think this is silly, and I suppose it is, but I missed the Control Tower. Jim and I smoked the bees into a stupor that Saturday and broke it all down, just like Elizabeth suggested. We left them three supers, nowhere near enough room for so many bees. And we caged the queen, to keep her from laying for a week, cut down the size of the hive. Bees, except queens and drones, live four weeks, maybe a little more in spring. A small mesh cage, with the queen and a half dozen attendants, fits in the top of the hive, so the bees can have their ruler nearby, but she can't get to the combs to lay brood. Coop her up for a week and the population will drop by a quarter a few weeks down the line.

When the smoke cleared and the bees rousted them-

selves, they seemed forlorn. Few foragers ventured out.
For a hive packed tighter than a cluster, they remained very
quiet. It made my heart ache to see that they felt the loss as
keenly as I did.

22.

Friday night, when Elizabeth came home, we had a cele-
bration. Growing up as I did, I learned to give thanks for
even the smallest peace. You know how sometimes you get
to the end of the day and say it was a stupid day. The bits
and pieces don't fit, like assembling a ceiling fan and finding the plastic packet of bolts didn't come with nuts. From
the inside, it felt like a stupid week, nothing going right,
never enough time, never enough of anything.

So when I called Elizabeth and she told me she'd be
home in time for dinner and not have to go back to work
that night, I planned a private party. On the way home I
stopped at the Red Sea, her favorite Ethiopian restaurant,
and ordered food for half a dozen, an excess of everything
she loved. I snagged a bottle of chilled Möet from the liquor store downstairs.

She beat me home for the first time in recent months and
I heard the shower shut off as I locked the door behind me.
We keep a picnic blanket in the front hall closet and I spread
that on the living room floor. I arranged the food on a
couple of the large crystal platters Elizabeth already had
when we moved in together: a layer of enjira, the flat
spongy bread Ethiopian food comes with, and gigantic
mounds of chicken in berber sauce, chickpeas and egg-

plant, okra with nuts, all separated by cigar-rolls of that sweet and sour bread. I filled the bucket with ice for the champers and set out two glasses.

She must have heard me then because she called my name. "You hungry?" I answered.

"Starved."

I kicked off my shoes and pulled a chair up close enough to lean back against it. I called out, "I have a craving for Ethiopian." She came in, her hair wrapped in a towel, fists tightening the belt on her blue-and-green ikat kimono. The stupidness of the week ended when I popped the champagne at just the right moment, the perfect sound effect to her surprise party.

"Ron, you are a dream." She kissed me and sat on the other side of the platters, her back against the couch. I poured. She toasted, "To a quiet weekend."

"A quiet weekend!"

"There too much food here to eat."

"Not if we stay in all weekend eating it."

"Do we have to get dressed for dinner?"

"Aren't I overdressed already?"

She wrinkled her nose at me. "You're always over-dressed." I worried a split second she was ragging on my wardrobe, so poor next to hers, but I knew she meant something else. She rolled some chicken and berber in enjira and fed me. I did the same for her, but clumsily, so I got to lick some that dribbled around her mouth.

We ate and drank and played until the weird emptiness of the week became vague memory. We lay on the couch and cuddled, sipping the last of the champagne and trickling it back and forth in our kisses. I wanted to be inside her robe, nuzzling, kissing her all over. I asked her, "How was work?"

"Perfect. Perfect. Everything is going just as we planned. The General is there now. I think we're going to win this one big."

"Congratulations."

"Thanks."

"What can I give you for a reward?"

Her small hand danced around my zipper. "How about this?"

"Will you give it back?"

"Only when I'm done with it."

But before we could move, the phone rang. If I hadn't had the champagne, I would have felt the tug of the G-forces then.

23.

I volunteered to drive her to the Pentagon. While she dressed, I made coffee for the both of us, herded up the leftovers, tried to shake myself back into the week.

"The plan was simple, that was why it went so well," she told me in the car. "Lebanon is just the name we give to a patch of land where they grow and process hashish. That's the whole story. The valleys grow the stuff. The cities process it. The ports ship it. The Lebanese make money and have power according to how many valleys, how many processors, how many ports they control. All the presidents of Lebanon this century, and who knows how far back, they're all from big hashish families. They're gangsters, that's all.

"So we occupy the ports, we set up shop on the roads. All we want to do is confiscate the hashish we find, we're not there to attack. But if they bring pistols, we have machine guns; they have machine guns, we bring tanks; they get tanks, we sink their boats. It's gangsterism, but it works. All we want to do is talk to them. We need their land, we need their connections, but we can't get them to talk.

"They want weapons from us. We can't give them weapons, what with the balance of power in the Middle East. And we can't invade them. We can't even have the Israelis invade them for us, though they'd love to. We tried it, sort of; it didn't work. And with the hostage situation, its a PR trap. Any time you go into Lebanon, the news comes out dirty. The only hope is some negotiated peace between the factions, under our protection. We get the land, we get the connections, they keep their hashish.

"It was working, you know, that's the thing. In not even a week, it worked. The Sixth Fleet has fourteen tons of hash in its holds right now. But who can the Lebanese complain to? So they agreed to talk. The press gave us ten days' grace, ten days' silence to see what we could do. I think we would have made it."

She fell into silence herself now. I didn't know what to say. She'd scrunched herself against the door, knees up, arms crossed against her chest. I put my hand out to her, patted her shoulder. "You'll work it out. I know you will." I smiled at her. "I have faith."

She took a deep breath and sat up. As we crossed the Potomac on the bridge near the Jefferson Memorial, I saw her come out of herself. Elizabeth is so small, really, but her presence enlarges her. Her brains, her beauty, her poise, they just come together to make her a much bigger force that your glance would credit her. On a football field, it's size or speed that matter. Excluding luck, you can figure out the winner on the track and in the weight room before the game. But in the games of the world, you can't just add up the parts. You have to put them together right. As I drove, Elizabeth assembled herself, and I felt like getting up and cheering for her. She'd handle whatever emergency came across our phone lines.

"Elizabeth," I said pulling through the gate, "can you tell me what happened?"

She sniffed once. I thought I detected a growing rumble inside her, like I heard in her father. She felt so big beside me, whatever news she told me came straight from heaven. "I guess it will be in the papers soon enough. The General went in to negotiate with one of the Muslim families, but he didn't come out."

"They kept him?" My voice felt like an animal noise in my throat, like a bleat or a squeal. "Hostage?"

"No," she said, opening the door. "They killed him."

24.

The news didn't reach the papers until Monday, but the press made up for their silence with screaming headlines then. I saw on the newsstand a New York tabloid screeching, *"DOUBLE-CROSSED!"* with a picture of some masked Lebanese gunmen. The more sedate papers, like the *Post* and the *Times*, covered the news on the front page, but saved their editorializing for the smudgy middle.

Of course, everyone released the same basic story. We offered Beirut secret negotiations aimed at establishing a large U.S. base on their territory, thereby introducing a handy force for peace in the Middle East. Elizabeth got no mention in this, of course; but neither did hashish, gangsterism or what amounted to our invasion of Lebanon. The General, leading the negotiations, went to the country estate of Lebanon's former president. The entourage reported gunfire. The General did not come out.

Only the better papers reported there was no proof—no

film, no message, no body—that the General had died. The evidence of ambush overwhelmed proof.

The press called for stern action against Lebanon.

The Secretary of State met with the President and the Joint Chiefs. He announced Wednesday afternoon that he asked "all hands to study all the alternatives. We will not let this outrage go unheeded."

Friday, a plane crash pushed Lebanon off the front page. Nearly a hundred people killed when a plane missed the runway. I checked the list of passengers, but my father wasn't among them.

25.

I hardly noticed I had worked that week. Friday, we had our monthly division meeting of Housing Characteristics, and I kept myself characteristically quiet. My office compiles figures on types of new housing: how many units of what type in how many buildings. Very little new happens. People seldom create new categories of buildings; the hardest part of our job is keeping track of conversions. Say if a small town in Massachusetts allows its old mill to go from light industrial to unrestricted zoning, and someone spends a bit of money fixing the old place up for loft living, we like to know. So we review zoning and bank records from all over, not only to include new construction in our statistical description of how we live, but also to look for hints that someone in Oregon has insulated their garage to rent as a studio to a student, or that houses in the small towns of Appalachia stand empty.

Most weeks, I notice work. My department must perform well or the census flounders. The census takers need accurate addresses—not names, just housing units—or they can't produce accurate population figures. Most people don't know that computer technology started in the Census Bureau. So much information: what's the use of it if you can't compile it, line it up on matrices, look at it another way.

Human social organization has never been so complex that we can't program a computer to sort it out. Not in my department, of course. We just do our small part. The Census Bureau uses computers, invents computers almost, but to the rest of the government we are a computer, a storehouse of information to be called up at will. My department is one chip in the hardware, and I'm the solder wiring it to the whole.

"Stutzer, anything to report from New Housing? I didn't get your report for the month."

Mr. Bienenkorb, my boss, chief of Housing Characteristics, never seems certain he's awake, as though maybe he dreamed up the Census Bureau and everyone inside it and at any moment the scene might switch to something else. "We've had a number of people out on sick-day these past two weeks, sir," I said. "I'm afraid we've dropped behind. The report is in a draft on my desk, but my secretary has been out."

"Well, I'm sure you would have said something if anything important happened this month."

"Yes, sir."

His heavy eyes searched me for a moment. I felt strange, alien. I was the youngest person in the room, except for Mr. Bienenkorb's secretary, Nancy, who I think was his niece. Everyone else used these meetings to lobby for more funds for their department, more computer time, more importance in the hierarchy. My mind couldn't handle what it had. I wanted to know what Elizabeth knew; I wanted to be beside her, inside her. I wanted to feed and groom her.

"Next month," my boss said, "find something important. Otherwise we'll suspect you're getting satisfied."

"Yes, sir." He sighed and looked to the next name on his staff list.

26.

"Are you coming home tonight?"

Elizabeth didn't answer at first. I stayed late Friday night to write the monthly report I lied about at the meeting. Here it was six-thirty, light still exploding in the DC sky, and the office, city and phone lines quiet as a winter hive.

I said, "It's OK, Elizabeth. You don't have to. Do you feel you have to be there?"

"No, no. I've been here overnight most of the week and nothing has happened. It's Friday here and Sabbath there and nothing will happen." The phone hissed with our breathing. "I'll be home before eleven."

"Is there anything I can get you?"

"Sleeping pills," she said, though her voice lulled like night-talking. "A very big bottle."

"That's no way to talk."

"A joke, Ron."

I know, I wanted to say, but the words stuck; I could never bring myself to slight her, even to defend myself. "Any closer to a solution?"

"We'll talk later. There is no solution. There's only goals and means. We don't even know what the goals are now."

"So you'll be home by eleven. I'll have a pizza sent around then."

"No pepperoni."

"I know."

"I can't sleep after pepperoni."

27.

I got home just after nine and the phone was ringing. It was Jim.

"I expected your machine. I wasn't sure any people lived there anymore."

"You might be right."

"Been working?"

"Yeah. Elizabeth will actually come home tonight."

"That why you haven't called me back?"

He had left two messages that week. The weekend before I had screened calls down to Elizabeth, her work and my family. Even Jim I couldn't deal with. "I can't tell you what kind of week it's been."

"Her work getting the better of you?"

"Me *and* her. Been in all the papers."

"I never read news, you know that. Are we invading Mexico?"

"Mexico? No! Why?" I was afraid I'd said too much.

"I got a postcard from Amy, remember the Oberlin girl two years b-b-back? She's thumbing around Mexico. I would hate for something to happen to her."

"What's new with the Tower?"

"You don't care about Amy?"

"Jim, *you* don't care about Amy. I'm supposed to?"

"I still don't want us to invade Mexico," he laughed. "The swarm cells have come back."

"You busting 'em?"

"Nope. I don't really have the time, with the spinach and peas coming in now. Do you want me to?"

"I don't know."

"They're going to go."

"How long has it been?"

"Where's your head? Two weeks Sunday."

We stole a week from the queen. Jim released her Monday, his first message that week. Then it takes twenty-one days to raise a queen, another week for her nuptial flight. Second week of June before they go. "How's the queen laying?"

"Like her life depended on it. Her bees been testy, so maybe it does."

"They're going to get sick if they don't spread out."

"Bee plague, might spread to the other hives."

"Can you rig up some supers around the property? Maybe they'll swarm into our own hives."

"I did that already. I told you." The second message.

"Oh yeah."

"You all right? Everything OK with Lizzie?"

"It's crazy here. Can't tell you why yet. Can I call next week?"

"I don't like it."

"I know."

"After nine. I'm in after nine."

28.

Elizabeth came home right when the pizza arrived. I had had a couple of hours to plan how I was going to put the brakes on. I couldn't do anything about my father. I couldn't do anything about the bees. But at least I could find out what was happening with Elizabeth. I figured we'd eat the pizza, drink a beer or two, and I'd draw her a bath. Then while she soaked, she'd tell me. She loves when I shampoo her. So I'll wash her hair and ask: What's going on?

But her first step in the door she says, "You won't believe what's been happening."

"What?"

"Today I met with the Secretary of Defense, the Secretary of State and the deputy director of the CIA."

"Are you sure you can tell me this?"

"What did you get?"

The pizza. "Olives, onions and peppers." I followed her into the bedroom. "Elizabeth, are you sure it's all right to tell me about this?"

"Is there someone else you would rather I tell?" she chirped. "I'm going to take a quick shower. Why don't you put the pizza in the oven and come sit in the bathroom so I can tell you what's been going on."

I know Elizabeth did not just walk in the door and assess my intentions. She's brilliant, more brilliant than I can understand, but she can't read my mind. She hardly even looked at me; her day, her week, her work filled her mind. Maybe she's right about instinct. My desire to know and her desire to tell erupted together, independently. I put the pizza in the oven, journeyed into the steamy bathroom and perched on the sink.

"I'm here."

She poked her head from behind the dusty-rose curtain. Suds dragged her reddish brown waves straight, but her green eyes sparkled underneath. They might have looked brighter because of the dark shadows under her eyes, part mascara, part exhaustion. She wrinkled her nose and pursed out a kiss.

I said, "So the two Secretaries and a spook."

"See? That's why I can tell you. You don't really care."

"About you I do."

"Thanks" bubbled from under the stream. "It wasn't just me, of course. The three of them met at Defense with military intelligence and the General's aide. They had been meeting for a while before they called me in."

She shut off the spigot. I handed her her towel as she pushed back the curtain. I always feel unspeakable pride when I see her like this, naked and glistening. She wrapped the first towel round her head and held her hand out for the second.

"You know that all week we have been struggling to figure out what went wrong. It has been rough on me, in particular. The General's aide came up to me Tuesday night, I was reviewing the game results on military exercises in the Middle East, the computer printouts. 'What are you doing here?' he says. 'It's almost midnight.'

" 'I don't want to take these out of the safe room,' I told him.

" 'Why are you bothering to look at them in the first place?' he asked me. 'Haven't you done enough already?' "

"He said that?"

"He's a solid creep. He sometimes thinks we're on different sides. That's the problem with military training; there always has to be an enemy. In international relations, the 'enemy' is just another point of view, a different set of priorities. I sometimes think I spend all my time telling soldiers to stop scratching their finger with the trigger.

"That's what jazzed me about this meeting. The first thing the Secretary of Defense tells me is, 'We have nothing to gain by military intervention.'

"Secretary of State says, 'We pulled our men out from the roads and the ports.'

"And the man from CIA says, 'We have almost certain information the General is not dead.'"

"He's not? That's great!"

"It's not exactly great. They still have him. We think." She exchanged her towel for the kimono and led the way into the kitchen. "Do we have any beer?"

"I picked up Pilsner Urquell. Seemed right for pizza."

"I want." She sat on one of the stools at the counter. That's where we have coffee in the morning and take-home leftovers. And pizza. The stools spin. Elizabeth pushed herself back and forth, stretching her bare feet into the spin. "So now we need another plan. Military solutions will prompt them to kill him. From their perspective, taking the General just evened the odds. If we threaten, they kill him. Now, if we want to negotiate, we both have fall-back positions."

"Those people sound crazy." I pulled the pizza out of the oven. The cardboard box had just begun to blacken at its edges. "The whole thing sounds crazy."

She looked at me like I *tried* to not understand. "But you see, at least they want to negotiate. This is good."

"I thought you told me last week they wanted to negotiate. And then they took him."

"They didn't like the terms of the talks. Who can blame them?"

"So what happens now?"

"This is the great part. We need a military presence without the threat of one. Someone who can figure out first-hand what it would take to win what we thought we had won before. But it can't be someone in a uniform, or even someone who looks like they belong in a uniform."

The pizza steamed as I separated one piece from the next. I slid the slice onto a glass plate. Elizabeth raised the plate above her head, so she could look at the pizza from below. I poured her beer into one of the uneven blue glasses she'd gotten in Mexico. I took a piece of pizza for myself. "Why no uniform?"

"The way they think our government works, we have an army and we have civilians. Civilians negotiate, armies invade. They don't want to negotiate with invaders."

"So now it's out of your hands, right? Over at the State Department?"

"Yes and no." She edged the tip of the pizza over the rim of the plate and held the plate up to her mouth. "I've been temporarily assigned to the State Department. I'm going to Lebanon as a part of the delegation."

She took a bite from her pizza. I took a bite from my lip.

29.

Elizabeth didn't leave until Monday, but we didn't have the weekend to relax together. She needed to spend half of Saturday being briefed on State Department priorities and procedures and half of Sunday at a meeting to decide, as she told it to me, "why the hell we want to talk to those creeps anyway." That was the first time I can remember not having to ask Elizabeth what she meant when she told me about her work.

The remainder of the weekend we shopped. I had never shopped with Elizabeth, not really. Grocery store runs, sure, and once to a clothes store when she wanted me to perk up my wardrobe and we ended up with a few ties and shirts I wear to please her. That I make more than my father does pleases me, but I'm still a civil servant, and I can't be spreading my money so thinly.

I grant we didn't have the time to comparison shop, but I don't think Elizabeth would have even if she had nothing better to do. We went to a store which doesn't advertise and which has no sign on it. Women less beautiful than Elizabeth modeled clothes for her. She didn't look through racks, but through books of very recent 10×12 photographs. The older women who advised her brought us tea and cookies and called me Mister and her Miss. She ordered three dresses, with certain variations from what the photos showed; the store, salon, boutique—I don't even know what to call it—had her measurements on file. The ladies qualmed a little, but finally agreed to deliver the dresses by Monday morning. To my eye, the clothes didn't look much different from what hung on the discount racks Elizabeth disdained, clothes you pay a tenth the price for and walk out with that day.

At least the shoe stores priced their wares where you could see. Elizabeth spent $500 there for three pairs, a flat sandal, a heeled one and black pumps. All I could think, carrying her bags through the familiar drugstore aisles as Elizabeth picked up stockings and Q-tips, was: That's almost $100 a shoe! Doesn't make sense, of course. Only unfortunates wear one shoe.

We came home exhausted, but forced ourselves to study. I felt unutterably alien cuddled under the covers with Elizabeth. Not only was this woman jetting halfway around the world to perform tasks which made no sense to me, she would do it with luggage valued beyond what my mother made in a year at the job my father beat her for having. Was I alien because I had come so far from home? Or because I could not recognize home, even lying in its arms?

Sometimes—very rarely—a bee will get lost and seek

shelter in a strange hive. Most often the guard bees will jump the intruder and that will end it. But it does happen that the bee might be allowed to join the new hive. She will work inside the hive until she loses the smell of her old home and then continue to perform the foraging her age suits her to. What does she think when she catches a whiff of an old hive mate on the stamen of a rose? Does she fill herself with nectar and huddle into the petals, waiting for night to come so the flower will close and cover her up?

30.

Monday I went to work late. I didn't want to see Elizabeth go, but she needed my help to make her trip possible. I could say now that I had some deep foreboding, but it wouldn't be true. I never liked it when she left, of course; but what made me feel the worst was watching her go. Maybe I felt like that's how I would feel when she finally left for good—maybe that's why I never complained when she called from work to say she had to leave town. But she needed me, and so I stayed, accepted deliveries, drove her to the State Department, kissed her good-bye.

I felt fierce the rest of that day and all of Tuesday. I reworked all the mistakes my people made. Usually I did that after work, so they wouldn't notice, wouldn't feel bad. But the start of that week, I took things off their desks, redid them in a red pen and handed them back. By Thursday morning I had splattered enough red ink to color a good-sized sea, corrected everything I could correct. Since I saved the newspapers for the night now, my way of spending time with Elizabeth while she was gone, I had to fill my work-time with work. My fierce energy, though, had put me days ahead and so when everybody cleared out for lunch my desk was broad and open as a winter field. I stared at the phone ten minutes before picking it up and calling information in Ohio.

I hadn't even realized I had been thinking about Dad, but I must have been. I didn't call my mother or any of the other family out there who might have known what had happened to him. I called the factory where he worked all his life. I wanted to know what they made of his disappearance.

The personnel office did the right thing, I suppose. They wouldn't tell me a thing. "I'm afraid that's confidential information."

"I'm asking about my father. Is it still confidential?"

"Unless we have Mr. Stutzer's permission to release employment information, we could be in violation of his civil rights. I'm sure you appreciate that."

I appreciated it. I appreciated that if I didn't get some news soon—about my father, about Elizabeth—I would explode. "Of course," I said. "Do you think you could get me in touch with Mr. Hamlin?"

Irv Hamlin had been my father's savior throughout his terminal employment with the company. He went to bat for him on the desk job when other people would have canned him. I had talked with him two or three times about my father. He took me out for a drink in the middle of the afternoon once when I was in college.

"We have an obligation to a long-term employee like your father," he told me. "Sure, he's going through a rough patch, but where else can he go? If we see him over this terrain, he'll stick with us when he gets his footing back." That stuck with me as I became a supervisor myself. No one's perfect, but supervisors have to be a little less imperfect. We can't really save anyone, but a little sympathy can turn into a lot of hope for someone in trouble.

The phone clicked back to life. "Ron Stutzer! How have you been? Keeping the wheels of government spinning?"

"Just sprinkling a little grease around."

"Good, good! To what do I owe the honor?"

"Mr. Hamlin, have you heard from my father?"

"Heard from him? What do you mean?"

"He showed up here two weeks ago, the middle of a workday, and then just disappeared."

Irv said nothing for five long seconds. I had been noticing myself and others falling into silence lately, as though we were all priests stunned into ignorance by the sudden revelation that God looks more or less like a virus. "Irv?" I prodded. "Mr. Hamlin?"

"Irv's all right." His voice embraced me less. He whispered now, like a comic-book spy into a watchband walkie-talkie. "I want you to know there was nothing I could do, Ron. I can only reach so far, and your dad went beyond."

"I understand. What did he do?"

He let out a whistling sigh. "Must have been a month, six weeks ago. He went up on the catwalk above the plant floor and hurled a crowbar into the grinder. The teeth splintered. Two people got hurt, metal flying everywhere. People could have been killed. We were just lucky."

"A crowbar?"

"Yep. Regulation crowbar."

"Could it have been an accident?"

"Mhm-mhm. Nope. Your dad knows that machine; he was the first person we trained on it. We built a plexiglass screen under the catwalk to prevent just this problem. No one saw him throw the crowbar, but after the accident he was sitting up there, legs dangling down, over to the side where he could get a good pitch into the well. I don't know what came over him. He wouldn't tell me a thing. I was so damned angry with him I could hardly talk myself."

"So what happened?"

"We put him on disciplinary leave. I heard he spent the whole day at Judy's"—the favored bar near the plant—"and left when the shift let out. I'd guess he was hiding out from your mother, but I don't know. How is she doing?"

"I don't know. I got nothing from her."

"What can she say? My youngest son got arrested for breaking into someone's house last year. Seventeen-year-old kid gone deaf on metal rock. All I wanted to do was crawl into a hole. Someone you love does something bad you can't understand, you look around for a place to hide."

"So what happened?"

"Gave him a year's probation, but I still think he has a drug problem. That's why he was breaking in: to get money for drugs."

"I meant my father."

"Oh, yeah. Sorry. We have an early retirement plan, starts July 1 of the year the employee turns fifty-eight. He'll be fifty-eight in October, so we agreed to keep him on the payroll until the end of June, provided he didn't come back. We've been mailing the paycheck to your mother for years, you remember when I set that up, back when you were playing ball. After that, we haven't heard from him. I can't tell you where he's gone."

31.

The newspapers buried the reports on Lebanon in the second section, articles bigger than newsbriefs but not much more informative.

They revealed doubts that the General had actually died.

He might be dead. That was as much qualification as they offered.

The press reported the opening of negotiations. A small delegation from the State Department arrived Tuesday for meetings with various officials.

The Israelis moved a couple of tank battalions to the northern end of their little country. "We are not worried about a military invasion," the local commander told a reporter. "We are worried about an invasion of refugees."

A scientist at the University of Texas in Austin discovered that a small amount of topically applied hash oil suppresses autonomic reflexes. "This might have application for coughs, allergies, even brain dysfunctions," he said.

A new Lebanese restaurant opened in SoHo, New York, to a warm review.

The portion of the Sixth Fleet which had been running maneuvers south of Cyprus returned for refueling and refurbishing to Suda Bay, in northwestern Crete.

Thursday, our softball team practiced for the first time; Jim couldn't make it. We look ready to beat the league this year. First game Saturday.

32.

Friday morning, I found a memo on my desk from Mr. Bienenkorb: Come see me around ten-thirty. My boss' imprecision always seemed odd in our line. Why not *at* ten-thirty? Before the meeting I had Virginia type up a report that wasn't due for a couple of weeks. Since my fury had put me ahead of schedule, there was no harm in letting Mr. Bienenkorb know.

"Sit sit sit, Stutzer. Take a seat." He closed the door behind me.

I handed him the sheaf of freshly typed paper. "The report on zoning change processing. I don't have the charts typed up yet. That's always time-consuming."

"Very good." He had a pair of half glasses he wore at the tip of his nose. To read, he had to crane his head back, like a man not sure of what he'd just heard or seen. Mr. Bienenkorb was in his mid-fifties and perpetually uncertain. "Looks all right." He surveyed the front page again, not reading, just surveying. "All right."

"It's only a draft, of course. I expect to make changes."

"No one's reading for style, Ron. I wouldn't worry about it much."

"But still . . ."

"Uh-huh." He leaned his elbows on his desk, hands together, and pressed his lips to his forefinger. Again the silence. At last he said, "Does it ever worry you how easily things can go wrong?"

"Wrong, sir?"

"You see, I started out looking to make my way in business. But in college I found out I didn't have near the motivation of the real biz-ads—that's what we used to call the guys in Business Administration, biz-ads. Nice ring, don't you think?"

"Yes, sir."

"So I turned toward accounting. Let them chase the dollars, they're more likely to catch them anyway. I'll just count them up, make sure they're in the right place. I took the civil service exam during school, so I could get a summer job, and after graduation I took a job in the Small Business Administration. Just my speed. I wanted to do that for just a little while, learn the ropes while I prepared for the CPA exam." He picked up a pencil. He kept fifty of them in a cup in his desk, all different lengths, but each sharpened to the quick. He surveyed the tip through his glasses. "I never got to take the exam."

He left a blank for me to fill. "Why is that, sir?"

"I met a girl who believed in government as a civilizing force. CPAs did not impress her. Government officials did. I stayed with government, compiling statistics for this and that and the other. And I'm glad. You know why?"

"Why, sir?"

"A couple of reasons. I like the fact the statistics are so forgiving. With a couple million numbers to add, a little mistake this way or that won't make a difference. It's not that way with tax returns, let me tell you. I never even do my own. I also ended up marrying that girl. I could have been a lot richer if I married someone else. Who's to know? I could also have ended up having a heart attack on the thirteenth green because every single tax return I filed got audited. So who can say?"

"Not me, sir."

"So what's been messing you up for the past month? You meet a girl?"

I never let people at work know about Elizabeth. That's one reason I call her instead of her calling me. And it's hard to be a boss if your people know that your girlfriend is much richer and more powerful than you. People just don't take you as seriously. So I never talk about Elizabeth, even to Mr. Bienenkorb.

"Not exactly."

"Is it something family? I heard about your father's visit."

"Nothing has changed there, sir. Nothing different."

He stretched back in his chair and laced his fingers behind his head. "You've been a good worker, moved along the old civil-service conveyor belt pretty fast."

"Thank you."

"Nothing but the truth. So why the change these past few weeks?"

"A lot of little things."

"That's what I was saying before. Little things change big things. I don't want to force a confession out of you, Stutzer. You got a problem, you can tell me, that's all."

"Nothing I can't handle."

"I'm sure that's true. But if you're beginning to think you might want to handle it with somebody, instead of alone, come talk to me."

"Thank you, sir. I will."

"Now get back to work."

33.

Saturday coughed up a cool misty rain. Never fails we play the first game of the season in a winter mist, no matter how summery the weather got before. We pony up our own money to play in this league, instead of getting some local business to sponsor us the way most teams do. But that's because we're mostly former athletes; half a dozen of us played in the pros and the rest for major college teams. We still don't win all the time, playing mushball against the blue-collar killers, but we intimidate the hell out of them with our uniforms, which have our names on the back and our team name—The Ex-Greats—on the front.

Jim got me onto this team. We get a few new players every year through our clubhouse network. Two or three of the guys still work in professional sports, in coaching or broadcasting, and another few work the college and high school circuit. With so much firepower, it seems funny we lose at all, but that's how it goes in sports: you train to take advantage of chance. If it worked out that better teams or players always won, there would be no sport. Same thing if it all depended on chance. We have the athletes, but the other teams train more together. When we win, we feel we ought to have, and when we lose, we blew it.

So I get the most satisfaction sitting in the dugout, waiting for my turn to bat. I watch the ritual patterns danced out by men in uniform, a complex social order which makes no sense without a rule book. When I first started keeping bees I could easily get the same thrill, sitting back and watching their movements. They seemed so repetitive I knew they must fit pre-set rituals, but I didn't know what they were. As I learned, I lost my wonder. But watching softball, I never lose my wonder. I think that, because when people play, I can't ascribe the whole thing to instinct, like I can with the bees. It's a mystery.

We won the game handily, 11–2, 11–3, something like that, in part thanks to moist air, which made the ball slippery. I had a couple of hits. I've become master of the hard stroke, a slick drive through the infield. Weekend players seldom muster the reactions to cover a hard-hit ball and throw it on target. One of my shots went through the third-baseman's legs and rolled around the left fielder two or three times before he made a wildly inaccurate throw. I made it all the way home on the error.

When I got to the bench, Jim said, "F-f-fine hitting." Even his uniform pants had a worn spot on the left thigh.

"Just trying to hit it where they is."

"How's my Lizzie?"

"She's gone."

"Gone?" He turned to stare at me. "Not gone gone?"

"Just gone."

"Work?"

"Yeah, of course, work."

He sniggered. "Don't scare me like that, man. Where'd she go this time?"

"Middle East." I figured so much went down there he couldn't tell where I meant.

"Not Lebanon!"

"I didn't say Lebanon."

"I heard sad shit about that place. I hope to hell she's not there." I didn't respond. Jim had to get up on deck. He walked out of the chain-link cage they set up for the teams and grabbed his black bat from the wooden rack. Taking a couple of swings he said, "The first of the new queens is p-p-pupating. She looks tough."

"How can you tell?"

The batter hit a high fly, certain to make the third out. "She wears her fur in a Mohawk. Get my glove, will you?"

34.

The rest of the weekend I felt sorry for myself. I should have trucked out to the farm to see what had become of the Control Tower, harvest honey, tend the hives the bees already tended in a way that suited them more than anything I could do. But instead I wrapped myself in a blanket and stared at sports on TV. I used to do that every now and again, before I met Elizabeth, but since we've been together—even when she was out of town on a weekend—I don't do it. There's always so much I can do for her: make a lasagna for the week, fix faulty plumbing, just attend the details of life she's mentioned don't suit her. But Sunday I felt like getting lost, like disappearing in the great wilderness inside. I wanted winds to pierce me, rain to soak me, trees and mountains and clouds to mock me. I wanted to shrink small as I could. I wanted to close myself in my cell and disappear.

Monday morning I discouraged myself by waking up and muddled through the day hoping to make Tuesday different. It was, very. I woke early and alert, bought papers from around the world and sat at my desk before eight. The day flowed like a thousand others had before I'd slid into this unsurfaced month. Calls came in, problems erupted and resolved, and hours blistered along like fire in dry wood. The wintry weekend disappeared in a hot flash, the rare perfect summer day Washington gets only in May and September: high in the eighties, a blue-glass sky studded with clouds of magic-act smoke.

Just before six, I parked my car around the corner from home and strolled out to the market. I figured to make myself a happy dinner: steak and onions, fresh spinach salad, a baked potato. I could see Jim sitting on the entry steps to my building as I rounded the corner. He saw me too and ran to meet me.

"I came as soon as I heard," he wheezed. "How are you d-d-doing?"

"What's the buzz? You look like you've been mainlining coffee."

"You haven't heard?"

"Heard what?"

He took the bag from me as I dug out my keys. "The n-n-news, the news!" He bumped into me pressing through the door. "Lizzie! They got Lizzie!"

35.

The phone was ringing as we walked in the door. I heard a long distance click and decided without evidence, It's Elizabeth, calling to tell me she's all right. A woman's voice came on, not Elizabeth. "Mr. Ronald Stutzer?"

"Yes, yes."

"Hold the line for Mr.———." Elizabeth's father.

Four bars of a Muzacked version of "Norwegian Wood" hissed in from New York before the Grumbler got on the line. "Stutzer? Ron? Have you heard the news?"

"Just this second. A friend told me, I don't really know what happened."

"I thought you might be able to tell me."

"No, sir. Last I heard—"

"I'm coming down to Washington tonight. You can meet me tomorrow morning at the Imperial Hotel, make it eleven-fifteen. Ask at the desk for me, I'm not sure which suite they've got me in. I'm talking to people at Defense and State. I'll have some real news by morning, not that claptrap comes in over the TV. I'm going to solve this. You with me?"

"Of course. No question."

"Tomorrow, eleven-fifteen, Imperial."

Before I could respond, he hung up.

"Who?" Jim asked.

"Elizabeth's father. He's coming tomorrow." I collapsed onto the couch. "What happened? What am I going to do?"

Jim brought me a beer from the refrigerator, an Urquell left from my pizza with Elizabeth. "I was out in the fields. Got a Walkman I listen to, but the batteries are too low to run the t-t-tape player, so I was listening to the radio. The news came on and said the car carrying Lizzie got cut off. Men from one of the Muslim groups picked her out special. The radio knew who her father was. I guess the Arabs did, too."

"But why?"

"Ransom? The report I heard on the radio driving in made a lot of this group being Muslim and the other one Christian. I don't know."

"What other one?"

"With that General last week. I don't know. I don't understand any of this. I'm scared for Lizzie."

"Me too. So what do I do now?"

"What can you do?"

"Wait. See what her father wants. Wait."

"Why did she go there? I told you the place stunk."

"She went because of the General."

"The one who got killed?"

"Maybe not killed.

"I thought he got killed."

I shrugged. "He was Elizabeth's boss. That was her plan."

"Her plan got him killed? They sent her over as a punishment?"

"I don't think it works that way."

"So can we go over and get her out?"

"Who?"

"The Marines. I don't know who."

I pointed to the phone. "The big man is trying diplomatic channels."

"What else is he going to do? B-b-buy the fucking country?" I had never seen Jim so worked up. I thought he was going to punt the coffee table out the window. His limbs began to jangle, he paced the room. "We have to get her out."

"Who now?"

"Us. You and me. We can do it!"

"We can't do anything, Jim. It's ten thousand miles away! They have machine guns! We couldn't even get into the country, never mind get out with her, if we could find her!"

"How do you know? Tell me, how do you f-f-fucking know?"

"I read about it! I live with her! Why are you shouting at me!"

"I'm sorry, man. I'm sorry." Jim began to sob. His face swelled when he cried, stretched skin taut. He plopped himself down on the couch next to me and I put my arm over his shoulder.

"We'll do something," I promised him. "I don't know what, but we'll do something."

Like wait, I thought, and cry ourselves wrinkled, old, forever.

36.

"Bienenkorb, Housing Characteristics."

"It's Ron Stutzer, sir."

"Where are you?"

The clock read nearly ten. Jim and I drank late and I slept fitfully until sunrise, and then fell into a pounding sleep. "Home."

"Home?"

"You were right, sir."

"About what?"

"The problems, the girl."

"You could have told me before."

"There was nothing to tell before. The girl is the one who just got taken hostage in Beirut."

I knew the silence before it came, but I didn't know it would last so long. I waited, and waited. "You're not fooling me, are you, Stutzer?"

"No, sir."

"What are you going to do?"

"I don't know."

"You tell me if you need some time. We can do this day to day. You're telling the truth?" Now I used the silence; what could I say? So he said, "Call if you need me. Good luck."

"Thank you, sir."

37.

The Imperial is a classic hotel, rattly and overblown in gimcrackery and aging bellhops. Even the perky young woman behind the counter had dour eyes. "Napoleon Suite, Mr. Stutzer. Gregory will show you the way."

I wore a suit instead of my normal tie and sports jacket, but I still felt shabby once shown into the anteroom of the suite. A genial assistant, in a better fitting, cleaner, more subtly-striped suit, offered to get me coffee. He sat me in the low and comfortable leather love seat, which with a matching sofa and an ornately carved wooden chair made up the living room's conversation group. Elizabeth's father's voice came rumbling through the bedroom door in a series of incomprehensible grunts. A cup of coffee and a glazed bun appeared on the squat marble table before me, but I resisted. I didn't want a sudden handshake to catch me sticky-fingered.

Elizabeth's father surprised me just the same. The same aide who greeted me at the door—there were three equally well-dressed—knocked on the jamb of the open bedroom door. "Mr. Stutzer, sir."

The big man responded immediately, rolling out of the room, open hand reaching to me. I stood; he covered my hand with both of his. "Ron, Ron, how are you holding up?"

"I'm managing, sir. But how are you?"

He made a face which indicated he'd hardly slept. "As well as can be hoped. I've been on the phone for hours trying to find out what happened, trying to hatch a plan."

"Do you know something more than the news?"

"Much more, of course, but everyone does. The news only tells what everyone already knows. We have been lucky in one thing: the driver recognized the marks of the abductors. They're Muslims, not Shiite, less extreme than that. We haven't heard anything from them."

I half-hoped he'd cry, because I know how to handle tears. This startling efficiency left me stony, immobile. My hands trembled in my lap. I didn't dare sip the coffee, though the warm bitterness would have brought my tongue back to life.

"I spoke with the ambassador in Beirut, who was sympathetic and lying. I suspect they set her up for capture." My eyes showed shock. "International politics can be very dirty, Ron. Betsy knew that; she'd studied it long enough. But you know and I know that she never thinks the rules of the world apply to her. Her mother was much the same way. You know about the accident, what is it now, fifteen years ago? Just going too fast for her own good. At least the ambassador agreed to support our efforts, as long as they don't interfere with the day-to-day operations of our Embassy. That translates: expect nothing, no interference but also no help. So I've been working the domestic end. Are you still with me?"

I couldn't be sure. My eyes felt slick with glaze. I wanted my Elizabeth. I didn't understand what her father wanted. "I'm still in shock, sir. What are we doing here?"

"We're working to get Betsy home," he cried, a more genuine shock than my small protest. "Isn't that what you thought we were doing?"

I spluttered, "I had no . . . I couldn't . . . I . . ." I felt like I think Jim feels, fighting my mouth to get out words I already heard in my head.

He stared staples into me. "You're here to help, aren't you? I didn't misunderstand your relationship with my daughter?"

"No, sir," I erupted, "I will do anything to bring Elizabeth home."

"Good, that's what I'm counting on."

That's when the phone rang. One of the fine suits answered it. Elizabeth's father said, "From what I have learned, nothing will guarantee her release. We can only try—"

The suit interrupted with a hiss. "Sir! The vice-president!"

He excused himself to me and picked up the phone from the leather topped table beside the carved chair, which creaked under his twisting weight. "Howard?"

Howard Denton, I realized. The Vice-President. Not of the big man's company, but of his country.

"I appreciate that, Howard. Your people have been able to count on me in the past, and we've been able to count on you." Elizabeth's father nodded and grunted. "A cover, credentials and a hands-off policy." Another short silence, and an explosion: "Of course I realize this is at my risk. I've talked with State, I've talked with Defense. I'm briefed, but they won't give approval without a nod from your boss." He listened. "Not until Thursday night, maybe Friday."

The rumbles rose and fell for a whole minute this time. I noticed that the suit had not hung up the other phone and was taking notes on the conversation, the earpiece clapped hard to his head, the mouthpiece buried in his hair. The suit signalled affirmative and Elizabeth's father said, "Yes, I have that. I offered to carry State's next packet tonight, that's when we'd like to go. I hate to ask this, but I think you'll have to call the Secretaries personally, Howard; memos, channels, anything else will take too long. The President—" I swear I heard a polite interruption "—well, thank you, I hope it does too. Give my regards to Barbara and thank her for her concern. Right."

The two phones went down simultaneously. "How such a jellyfish of a man has got so far I will never know," the big man confided in me. "Higuera, call transportation, get the plane ready to fly. No sense pushing official clearance if we're grounded with technical problems." The darkest of the suits headed for the phone. "Do you know your Social Security number?"

"457–57–2028. Why?" The third suit wrote it down.

"We might need it, if you agree to help."

"I said I'd do what I can. What do you have in mind?"

He settled his bulk into the spindly chair and contemplated me. I believe he contemplated what he would tell me, and I guess he decided on the truth. "Ron, we believe that the people who took Elizabeth took her for political reasons. We also believe their politics have a price. They won't come forward to ask for a ransom, because they would lose face in Lebanon, but if Elizabeth 'escapes' and they find some money that same day, no one will know or care."

"I understand."

"Good. The problem remains that we don't know where

Betsy is, or who leads the kidnappers, or how to get in touch with them. We need a man on the scene. Government agencies won't handle it; Betsy represents acceptable losses in this chapter of US-Lebanese history. The private group we normally hire to do this work won't take the job, and they're frankly not much better to deal with than the people who took her. We need one interested individual to go to Beirut and bring Betsy home."

"Don't ask twice," I said.

"I knew I had the right man. We'll need your driver's license."

38.

I maybe had a minute here and there between buying supplies for the trip and packing up. Jim had called, left three messages, but I didn't call him back. The bank called to say that my VISA card had reached its limit but still kept turning up in stores and hotels; could I call them back. Well no, I couldn't. Elizabeth's father said his people would take charge of my mail, my work, my life while I was gone. I didn't expect that to cover my father or Jim or the Control Tower.

Ten of eight, the doorbell rang. I looked out the window and saw a silver limo floating above the rest of the traffic at the curb. I didn't buzz the driver in; I could carry my own bags. Didn't want to keep Elizabeth's father waiting.

39.

I have never understood how an experience so completely new can seem so completely familiar. I never rode in a limousine before, but the feel of the leather seats, the light diffused by the shaded windows and then scattered by three dozen tiny bulbs set in ceiling tracks, the position of the telephone and bar, the odd quiet of the radio and the road, all of it felt reassuringly like a place I'd been before. It's like being well thought of, like knowing you're loved, a liquid unreality as easy to accept as a pat on the shoulder and a down comforter.

"Most of what you need to know you will learn on the flight," the Grumbler told me, "but I have many years of expertise in giving advice, so I decided to do that part myself."

"I appreciate it."

"Wait until you hear it. You might not be so happy about receiving it." I nodded. "You are going to a strange land. No one really knows what went wrong there. Without social rules, no one knows what is right there. So you must trust no one, no matter how you would feel about them if you met them here.

"Weaponry will only get you in trouble. If you feel you need a gun, you will find a variety on the plane and someone there to instruct you on their use. Take one if you want, but my sense is you're more likely to get shot with it than to shoot it.

"Do not worry about expenses." He handed me an oaktag envelope. "These dollars should see you through; if not, banks still work in Beirut. I've sent ahead a photograph of you and arranged a personal line of credit.

"Stick to a ceiling of half a million dollars for the ransom. Start at fifty thousand and let them go up. I will have someone in the American Embassy in Tel Aviv at all times. If you need more money, backup or escape, call.

"If you get nowhere in ten days, come home. That means they are not interested in negotiations. They will know who and where you are before you do. They will let you find them if they want to tell us anything.

"Do you have any questions?"

"A million, but I don't know where to start." He laughed now, the round bag of money and prestige. His good humor confounded me. His daughter! Elizabeth! No fear? I had to admire the calm. Barely a day since the news broke and already the man had a plan and someone committed to its execution.

I had to smile too. I'm the executioner.

"That's it. You're going to have to relax. Lebanon is far away and you will need sleep." I squinted through the window and saw we were back at the hotel. "I'm not going with you out to the airport. I thought you might like the time alone, and some details still need my attention." The car stopped in front, and Higuera opened the sidewalk-side door. The noise, smell and light of the city trickled into the automotive version of self-confidence.

"I will do my level best, sir. I love Elizabeth."

"Of course you do, Ron, that's why you're here. But don't get yourself killed or captured over there. If you get back safe at least we haven't lost anything. No foolishness, no heroics." He took my hand and used my leverage to roll him up from the seat. I passed his hand to Higuera, who walked him out. "I expect to see you in two weeks, looking none the worse for wear," Elizabeth's father said, hand on the roof, bent at the waist. "Please don't disappoint me."

I couldn't answer. The door closed. The ghost driver beyond the tinted shield eased the car into gear and we floated away.

40.

Even at the airport nothing conformed to my experience. We drove to a far end of Dulles, a complex of buildings like a busy small airport off to the side of a huge inactive one.

But we didn't stop in any of the buildings, except the checkpoint at the gate. We drove, as clear as I could make out in the burgeoning dark, across the tarmac where the private planes slept. About fifty yards past the last of the small props sat a small jet. It bore no markings other than registration numbers: no logo on the tail, no characteristic colors, nothing out of the ordinary except the unbelievable ordinariness of flight. A dozen people hovered around the plane, stowing supplies and gassing it up. At the top of the fold-up stair, the Grumbler's light-suited man slowly swung the door back and forth on its hinges. As I stepped out of the car toward the trunk for my luggage, he chanted, "Stutzer! Mr. Stutzer! This way, Mr. Stutzer." The driver and one of the jump-suited loaders already heaved my bags out from behind. "Watch your step!" He had changed his suit for what looked to me like boating clothes. Flat canvas sneakers, light cotton twill pants and a summer-green polo shirt. He put his hand out half in support and half in politeness. "We didn't get introduced before. My name is Noah Jacobs. I'll be coordinating support in Israel. We have a cold buffet set up in the conference room."

He pointed through the open door to a cramped version of a boardroom: big table in the middle, comfortable high-backed chairs all around. Trays of food glittered. Inside, the plane looked just like the pictures I'd seen in brochures of expensive but rentable yachts, all dark wood and brass.

No ugly polyester curtains separated classes; rather a string of rooms trailed back into the tail. A short man with thick glasses and curly thinning hair fading black to white sat at the table sampling the goodies. A huge man with blond hair on his bare arms hulked against the wall and then seemed to laugh as I stepped in. The short man looked up at me when Jacobs spoke to him. "Professor Nusanti?" His eyes gave a twitch behind the lenses. "Please meet Ron Stutzer. He's the man you'll brief." Jacobs turned to me. "Professor Nusanti teaches at Columbia. He's the firm's independent expert on the Middle East."

When I was in college, I met with professors only when I needed a favor, and often as not one of the assistant coaches came with and actually did the asking for me. I never needed to plead to pass a course, but I always needed more time than I had to complete the work. I dreaded professors. I knew they knew I knew nothing.

The professor stood and shook my hand. "A week in Beirut and he'll be an expert too. You've undertaken a very difficult and dangerous job, Mr. Stutzer. I admire you."

Against the wall, the big man burrowed his fingernails into his scalp, as though our simple conversation meant something incomprehensibly horrible.

"Call me Ron, Professor."

His face opened in pleasure. "And my name is Ahmad. I recommend the asparagus wrapped in sturgeon. I'll eat the whole plate if you don't fight me for it."

The plate was a foot and a half around and piled high. The whole crew couldn't finish it. "Let's just divide it up now and use them for poker chips."

The professor laughed, "You didn't promise me a sense of humor, Mr. Jacobs. Come, Ron, sit down and let's talk."

41.

Before I could negotiate the chair next to Nusanti, the big man approached. "So you're going into Lebanon." His eyes were red, white and blue.

I looked to Jacobs. "Ron, this is Bengal." You could tell the name embarrassed Jacobs.

"Bengal?"

"Code name. He's our guerrilla warfare expert. He's getting off in Paris."

I shook Bengal's hand and mine got lost in his. "You're the one who will show me about the guns."

His big head rocked. Jacobs said, "Bengal knows everything about weapons. Not missiles, you know, just guns."

"And knives, string, staple guns, poison, slingshots, you name it."

"String?" He pinched his throat and gagged. "Ah," I said, "string."

"I did eight years in Nam, three in Argentina, three in Honduras, two in Afghanistan and the last half a dozen chasing trouble around the world for these bozos."

"Never played football?"

"Pansy game for college boys." But he smiled, like he wanted to play, just never did. "You never made it pro, right? I work with some guys made it pro."

"Yeah, not big enough, not fast enough."

He glanced at Nusanti. "Too much college learning."

"Maybe, yeah."

"Well, you go back to class. When you get done I'll tell you what you really need to know."

The professor told me all he knew about Lebanon, it seemed, about the people, the history, the land, the cities, the laws, the leaders, the pacts. We ate, we drank, I listened and worried: What will stop these people in quest of a peaceful home from gunning me down to get it?

That's what I asked Bengal after the professor gave up on me and went to bed.

"Nothing. They might shoot you for nothing at all."

"So why was I asked to do this job?"

"Because I won't."

"Why?"

"I set foot in that place I'm meat. I'm known and those guys have no honor. If I buy it in the course of duty, I can buy that, but just for stepping off a plane? Fuck no."

"So none of the professionals go?"

"Oh, you can find some crazy freelancers to do anything, even go to Lebanon, but the fat man don't want them working for him."

"Am I crazy to go?"

He eyed me. "As I get the story, you're in it for the fat man's daughter. Even that ass isn't worth Lebanon, so you must be in love with her. That's proof to me you're crazy. You want to learn something about guns?"

The new metal of the weaponry, harder than the jet's fuselage, reflected nothing, like my memory. I couldn't compare any part of the past day and a half to anything that had gone before. 'Before' never happened. Everything was now. Bengal. The professor's openness. Destination. The sturgeon. The plane. Everything my ears absorbed, my eyes lighted on, my mouth enclosed, I had never heard, seen, tasted before.

Bees, when left to their own will, never build supers and frames and so on. A swarm hunts for a cool, dark protected alcove—the hollow of a tree, a miniature cave—when they move away from home. But when a bee-keeper sets up a hive, the bees don't die from the strangeness of it all. They take the preformed frames as a blessed convenience and build from them. They guard the narrow entrance to the hive just as they would a propolis-enshrouded opening in the wild. When midnight came, thirty thousand feet above the ocean, I accepted Jacobs' offer of the master bedroom, where my bags had been neatly opened and my toiletries carefully laid out. I hardly had time to notice the perfection of the bed's cotton-and-linen sheets before a common sleep pushed all sense of strangeness aside.

42.

My long sleep must have pushed the strangeness not only aside, but into a pile, because when I stepped off the airplane I stepped right into it. Maybe back in the wild west, or today in some neighborhoods in American cities, people appreciate the authority of a gun, but I doubt observing other people wielding Saturday Night Specials has the same impact as a machine gun being used as a direction marker by a fifteen-year-old boy. Everywhere you look around the airport in Beirut, young boys in torn uniforms wave weapons around like sticks. If they want people to exit through a door instead of through the rubble, they point the little doughnut end of the barrel at you and they whisk it off towards the path they want you to take.

When a policemen comes into the convenience store while I'm there, looking for a cup of coffee and something sweet, I look at his face, his badge and his gun. My eyes linger on the gun a long time. Even tucked snugly into that thick leather holster, the polish of the metal speaks a kind of reverence for the power it has. We shine silver and gold, because they are powerful, but we don't polish raw steel except when we make it into a weapon.

American policemen are fit youngsters or experienced pot-bellies. Their faces communicate their authority. The badge and the gun only back it up. But the children of Lebanon have no authority except their guns. They're slight, dull boys, thrilled by the powerful impression the dark hole at the end of their weapons will make on a stranger. They toss the guns around, they rest their chins on the barrels, they scratch themselves with the sights. With their weapons, they are casual gods, guarding a country which announces at its border that nothing is safe and authority rests only on a trigger.

I had the chance to study the boys because the Lebanese did not want the plane bearing Americans on the the ground for long. We unloaded my bags and several crates of goods for the American Embassy and tucked them against what had been a wall. A boy-god sat on a high stone nearby, kicking his authority like a pendulum between his legs.

"I don't know what's keeping them," Jacobs said to me. "The Embassy people like to be prompt."

The professor sweated uncomfortably and tried to hide in the small available shade. Very nearly two days had passed on the calendar, but a quarter of that was time-zone shift. Early evening blistered off the tarmac. "I'll go inside and call," Nusanti volunteered. "I want a quick look around anyway."

The boy with the gun kept staring at us. "This place gives me the creeps," Jacobs muttered. His nighttime cliché, muttered in bright light, gave me the same feeling. He said, "You never know when something might blow."

"You've been here before?"

"Me? No. I don't like going places where you have to worry about your cab driver's connections."

An older soldier, in a better uniform and with his automatic handgun still in his cloth-and-metal holster, beleaguered the young guard until he got off the wall and stood more militarily. When the older one came over to us, I saw he was hardly twenty. I couldn't tell what the insignias he wore meant, but he had a lot of them. He spoke to us in clipped Arabic, or that's what I guessed it was.

"We don't speak your language." Jacobs tried gesturing what he said.

The adolescent major puffed once at us and then screamed, "Basbot! Basbot!"

"Passport?" I asked Jacobs.

"I guess."

I turned to open my small overnight case. Before I could bring my hand to the zipper I heard a thin metallic click. I looked back. The soldier had a very square gun in his very square hand. I pulled my hands back from the bag like it was made of acid. "My passport is in there." I pointed with one finger, my hands still withdrawn.

"Basbot!" he screamed again.

This time I moved slowly, like a dance of unpacking. My papers sat right on top, but it still felt like ten minutes getting them out. I never had a passport before I met Elizabeth. She wanted to take a vacation to Jamaica, so I went and got one. We never got to go, because something came up with her work. Now her work put it to use.

I handed over my virgin passport into which Jacobs had stapled a document saying I was attached to the US mission and had diplomatic immunity. I had no idea what good that would do me.

Even the major used his gun as a pointer, running it like a finger along the information in my passport. He didn't even unfold the diplomatic papers. He tapped my name twice and then prodded the crates with the toes of his boot. Boots! I thought, feeling my own feet burn through the soles of my loafers. I jumped when he barked at me and bumped against Jacobs. I felt him trembling through his cruisewear. The major barked again. Jacobs said, "I think he wants to search them."

"They're not supposed to, right? That's a diplomatic packet."

The man started kicking the crates. I understood the boots.

Just then the professor came out. He said something to the soldier in Arabic. The major whirled around to face the professor and, after a flash shock at this American face, the two began howling and gesturing at once. In a minute it was over. The major hurled down my passport and walked away, stopping by the young boy with the gun to send him over to us, and the professor explained what happened. "People use American and diplomatic IDs to plant bombs or transport weapons, he says, though I don't believe him. He knows Noah and I are leaving you behind; his real job here was to get us on the plane and out of here. Beirut is a small town, when it comes to Westerners. He said, 'This is no city for an American fool. He could die here.'"

The young boy came up close to the professor and said something sweet and high.

"Time to go," Ahmad told Jacobs.

"I'm Jewish," Jacobs told me, clasping me around the shoulder. "They don't like Jews here. Good luck."

"Good luck," the professor echoed. "Call if you need anything. The sergeant was right: this is a dangerous place."

Ahmad and Noah started to the plane. "Professor!" I called out. The boy blocked my way with the barrel of his gun. I could have removed his head with one arm, if it hadn't been for the gun. Fortunately Ahmad heard me.

"Yes?"

"Where's my driver?"

"Oh, yes! A little delay at a checkpoint. They'll be here very soon. And Ron?"

"Uh-huh?"

"From now on keep your papers in your front pocket. Out of sight, but no place you could hide a weapon."

I picked up my passport and sat down, chasing my

stares from the young god's gun to the departing plane. When Elizabeth's father's jet taxied away, I felt certain that time had stopped, that nothing came next. If, in some distant millennia, an interstellar traveller happened on earth they would find me just as I sat, surrounded by my crates and luggage, guarded by a child, and unspeakably alone.

43.

But a heartbeat after I lost sight of the jet, I heard my name. It came from a small muscular woman in a straight black skirt and a colorless blouse. Her eyes had an odd cast to them, as though they had been brown but lost interest and faded to beige. She had heat-brittle hair, burnished skin and a human smile, a relief from the boy-gods. I swear she was pound-for-pound as strong as me, though when I stood I dwarfed her. She put up a hand. "Andrea Kowalski. I'm military, but we don't wear uniforms here. Too dangerous. This all?"

"Just the two crates and my bags."

"The van's coming through the west checkpoint. Sorry it took so long getting down here, but no one in Beirut believes a van is just a van. It's a tank, or a carrier, or a bomb. Panel vans make good car-bombs; the shrapnel really flies. Do you have any idea where you are?"

"Outside of Lebanon, you mean?"

"I mean in Lebanon." She pointed past the guard and his gun toward the airstrip. "That's west; the Mediterranean is just beyond there. West Beirut is Muslim, East is Christian. You better have a good sense of direction or a good compass if you plan to stay here long."

"Not more than a week, if I can help it."

"They all say that. Here's the van."

Oddly, the boy with the gun helped Andrea, me and the driver Mahmet load up. We sat three across in the front and were waved through the gate off the field. After a couple of turns we mounted a wide and almost abandoned avenue clustered with low flat concrete and stucco homes. Every hundred yards or so, what had been a larger building glowered in a heap. Pretty little houses and big heaps gave way to a belt of rubble for almost a mile along the road. The avenue narrowed to a rock-strewn road, and we entered the checkpoint. Three gun barrels came in the windows as we stopped, and the faces behind them looked like they belonged to my airport guard's younger brothers.

Mahmet explained who we were and what we carried. I pulled my passport from my pocket too slowly for the elder boy at my window. His gun barrel came in right under my nose. I smelled dust and oil and powder. That gun had been fired, I would bet. He pulled the barrel back and pointed it at my face. I froze, a little metal zero aimed at my forehead.

"Pizpo! Pizpo!" the younger soldier said to me. I whipped it out and fumbled it over to the window. The elder turned his back on the van to look at the pages, but he kept one hand on his gun and the barrel in my face. The guard on the other side had already finished with Andrea and Mahmet. Mahmet raced the engine and untensed the clutch a hair. The van lurched forward an inch. My passport came flying back through the window, and we raced off into the afternoon heat.

"The Amal," Andrea explained. "Most of them can't read. They treat every passport like 'Dick and Jane.' Better keep it out; we got a few more checkpoints before we get home."

The American Embassy put me up in a small house in the compound, but just for the first night, Andrea explained. "We'll review your options tomorrow and find a hotel for you."

"There are hotels here?"

"They aren't all gone yet. None good, but they all have bars, unless Hezbollah closes one down for the night."

A deep rumble bounced around us, like the crash of a distant tidal wave. "What was that?"

"Car bomb, likely, but that must have been three, four miles away. Nothing to worry about. Wash, relax, sleep. I'll be back to fetch you in the morning."

44.

I had no idea what time it was when Andrea knocked on my door. My sleep had been either good or bad, I couldn't tell which. I might have dreamed the explosions and rumbles, in which case I slept horribly; or I might have woken briefly out of a coddling slumber when I heard them.

"Terrorists sleep late," Andrea said when I opened the door, "because they're up all night. You can tell the good people by the hours they keep, so wake up."

"Do I have to be alert to qualify for good?"

"Just awake. Got a meeting at six-thirty. Hustle a little."

"What time is it now?"

"Six thirty-five."

Andrea walked me down the compound paths. The buildings seemed to have grown out of the very dirt. Everywhere I looked I saw red-eyed soldiers wearing baggy fatigues. Even Andrea was in a bit of a uniform; the rare attentive soldier saluted her. The guarded compound seemed very small in the early light. The occasional tree, struggling up from the pale, clay dirt, made it feel smaller still. If all the buildings got shelled to oblivion, they'd still have to annex some territory beyond the walls to set up a football field.

The largest of the buildings skulked against the ground in the shadow of a wall. The sign by the door said 'Headquarters,' but they couldn't have tried to make the place less imposing.

Not so inside. The place sparkled. Every door bore a label. "I'll be in there when you get done," Andrea told me, pointing to the room marked 'Communications.' Three doors down across the hall we entered a room marked 'Commander.' "Lieutenant Colonel Harbison, Ron Stutzer. Ron, the chief."

I shook hands with a rail-thin man in his mid-forties. His eyes glinted as though freshly oiled. His hair had been reddish-blond in his youth and now fell lank and pale. He had no eyebrows to speak of.

"That will be all, Captain."

Andrea saluted. "Look for me later," she whispered, slipping out.

The chief eyed me silently and then walked behind his desk to his chair. The desk buried him in a corner, clear, I realized, of the only window in the room. Out the window, a yard beyond the screen, I saw remnants of hay stuck in the mortar of the surrounding wall. Tall grass grew between the window and the wall. I stood until the chief indicated a chair.

No sooner did I settle down than he stood up. His voice flowed smooth but strident, like an evangelist. "The United States government has recommended American citizens leave Lebanon. The State Department discourages travel here. I know how you came, but I can't say I endorse your presence here. We will help any American citizen interested in leaving Lebanon, but you have no interest in leaving. We will not help you."

"I understand."

He gravelled briefly, the best laugh he could scare up on

short notice. "You understand? Your friend thought she understood. Harvard coursework might fly high in Washington, but here it puts you in a stinking cellar chained to a bed, which is where I'd bet she is now."

"You know where she is?"

"If I knew where she was, I would not tell you. I said we wouldn't help you. That doesn't mean we'll try to get you killed."

I was about to say 'I understand' again, but changed my mouth mid-mumble. "I don't know where to begin."

"Oh, I thought you understood." Harbison leaned threateningly close to me, his tail against the edge of his desk, his arms crossed. "You don't know what kind of place this is. We're in the midst of an attempt to forge a new model for the people of Lebanon; that's why your friend and the General came here. Some people don't want peace. That's why those two got taken. How much money do you think it will take to interest them in peace? What do you think they will use the money for, if you can convince them you have enough to buy back your friend? The General personally oversees a budget of about six billion dollars. How much do you think it will take to buy him out?"

"I'm not here to interfere with your plans."

"I know what you're here for. I'm in the knowledge business, Mr. Stutzer. But unlike your friend Professor Nusanti, I know how valuable knowledge is. I never give it away. That's why I have more of it."

"You won't share any with me?"

He laughed again just like before, and I could tell now it was his sincere laugh, his stone-riot laugh. He went behind his desk and angled into his chair, still making sounds in his throat like he knew his laugh hadn't convinced me, like he was practicing how to laugh, so he could get it right next time.

"Mr. Stutzer, you might not realize it, but you are in a war zone. There used to be a country here, now there isn't.

This used to be an embassy, now it's a base of operations. I won't share anything with you except some advice. Trying to free your friend could get her killed, you killed, the General killed and our whole purpose here killed. You earned the right to get killed anywhere you want when you had the good fortune to be born on the way to Mercy Hospital in Ohio. But don't expect my cooperation in getting yourself killed, or keeping you alive, if it will hurt the interests of our government here. Now do you understand?" He didn't wait for me to respond, but hit his intercom. "Send in Commander Faid." Harbison ignored me on his way to the door. He left it ajar and then sat back down.

With the door a shade open, the man appearing behind it didn't know whether to step in or knock, so he did both. Harbison interrupted this awkwardness by shouting, "Don't stand around, Hussein. Come in, come in."

The man shuffled in clumsily; he seemed unused to shuffling. We were of a size and an age; even our moustaches looked alike. I stood and put my hand out to him. He took my fingers only and kept his eyes on the chief.

"Hussein, this is Ron Stutzer. Mr. Stutzer, Hussein Faid, a commander in the Christian Front. Commander means he in charge of about twenty-five blocks in East Beirut, one of two or three dozen commanders we know about. The Christian Front is not exactly an army, Mr. Stutzer. It's more like a private police force hired by the people in a particular neighborhood. We have taken over a number of abandoned houses in Hussein's quadrant; it's one of the nicer sections of Beirut, and Hussein and his men seek to keep it that way. We have decided to give you one of the smaller houses up in the hills, so you can save a bit on expenses. You might want to give Commander Faid half of what you would have spent in hotels. He offers the best protection in Beirut, if you decide you want to travel with a guard. A lot of people do."

Harbison stood, but stayed behind his desk. I could not help but realize I had to stand and leave with Hussein, my protector and my captor. "Don't forget to call us every day, Mr. Stutzer. We're busy people and this is a dangerous city. The only way we can be certain you are all right is if you let us know."

Hussein followed me into the hallway and shut the door. We stood shoulder to shoulder. Then his face wrinkled into a smile and bulged into a laugh. "That man is crazy," he said. His accent was more British than anything else.

"Crazy?"

"It is the right word?"

"I guess. I don't know him."

"He's very powerful. You had better stay in the house he has provided. You will be safest."

"And what do I owe you for my safety?"

"How much days you plan to stay here?"

"Ten maybe."

"And you bank in dollars?" I nodded. "It is simple then. One thousand dollars. If you will need a guard it will be more. I will take you home now."

"Let me stop here first." We were at 'Communications' and I wanted to know what Andrea thought of my arrangement. The door was locked, so I knocked. A young black face peered at me through the two-inch crack. "Can I talk to Andrea?"

He called back into the room. "Captain? A visitor!"

Andrea came to the door. As she swung it open to walk through, I saw a room arrayed with lights, huge maps on the walls, consoles everywhere. It was the first color I'd seen since I arrived. She closed the door behind her and leaned against it. "I see they put you under guard."

"I kind of got that feeling myself."

"It's not so bad, really. Just report in when you're going somewhere."

"Great. But where should I go?"

"With him first. I had someone pack your bags and bring them over; they're just inside the door. Then I'd get settled, recover from the trip and study your maps."

"And tomorrow?"

"Tomorrow, walk around town. Go to the beach. You want to meet me at the bar at the Paris Hotel tomorrow at six?"

"Sounds good."

"Good. Remember, keep your tail clean. People will be watching you."

45.

After Hussein took me up to the house, a European sort of cottage really, with wood beams and stucco and real glass in the windows; after he introduced me to the mixture of Lebanese and Aryan boys who carried their guns just like the ones at the airport and checkpoints, but who were supposed to protect rather than trouble me; after one last warning from a busybody neighbor not to go downtown if I didn't have to—after all this, I slept through the heat of the day, huddled away the rest of the day, and asked Hussein's boys to bring me food before bed. What else could I do? I felt trapped and I was captive, though under better circumstances than Elizabeth. The Christian Front spied for the US, I gathered, and the Christians who lived in the luxurious houses in the hills of East Beirut paid protection to the Front for the privilege of being spied on. Me too, I realized. Studying my maps in the warm dusk, I realized that I became a hostage the very moment Elizabeth did.

I woke—was it Sunday morning already?—from a fitful drowning sleep to a mixture of English and French wafting through the shuttered windows like distant bird calls. I dressed for the cool of the house and sweltered as I stepped out into the morning heat. The voices came no closer as I went out, but rather disappeared in the rumble of cars. Though the front of my small house faced a tangle of hilly roads, it backed against a ravine through which a main road cut. It tumbled straight out of the mountains into the center of town.

One of the joys of capture is that help is never far. Two boys in familiar fatigues sat in a jeep in the shade in front of my house. One of them spoke passable English. "How can I get into town?"

The two soldiers discussed it, and the one who spoke no English put the butt of his gun on the floor between his legs and bent over the muzzle to the radio. "We will call you a taxi," the partner said. "Have you a passport?"

I handed the passport to him and he studied it while the radio hissed and spat in Arabic. "You would do better without this sometimes," he said, flicking my commission with the back of his hand. "Take it out. Keep it apart. Then you will have it if it will do you good." He pulled a small notebook from an open compartment in the jeep's dash and compared my name to the list in the book.

Over his shoulder, I sighted my entry before he did.

★ *Ronald F. Stutzeir—$1000.*

I asked, "What's the star for?"

The boy yanked the commission out of my passport and folded it neatly. Handing both back, he said, "Because you are a special guest, Mr. Stutzeir. Please return before dark." They must keep their cabs waiting nearby, because a stone-age Mercedes rattled up just then. "You should see our beautiful beach. Check in with us when you come back tonight."

46.

My driver said, "I am Amir. Can you believe those clowns in their uniforms?"

"Are they clowns?"

"Anything in a uniform is a clown. In the circus you tell them by their clothes. It's the same in Lebanon."

"You speak English very well."

"I should. I majored in it in college. University of Massachusetts."

"What are you doing back here?"

"Your immigration service can be very diligent. I was born here." He shrugged.

"It must have changed a lot since then."

"What with the war?" My turn to shrug. "Sure, sure. But not so much the way you think. A lot of ugly old buildings blew up, one hundred thousand people are dead, half the population left, but the city still lives. You'll see what it's like downtown. That's where we're going, no?"

"There or the beach."

"Let's go to the beach."

So we drove on. The first checkpoint we hit was Christian Front. The guns came in the window, my passport went out, with my commission. As I took it back after a cursory review, Amir sped off. My arm, hooked over the front seat, kept me from rolling back. Once we were clear of the checkpoint, I saw him uncover his gun, which had been under an oily rag on the seat beside him. "I always carry this, but it doesn't help to show it at the checkpoint, especially with the Christian Front. They look down their noses at the rest of the militias, even the army." He made a spitting sound.

"So why do you work for them?"

Amir looked at me in the mirror. "Why do you say I work for them? No, you're right. Because here you must work for someone, and the Christians are much more calm than the Islamic Jihad or even than the government. People say the Christian Front has no passion for killing, and no remorse about it either. But if I am dead, why do I care if the man who killed me feels remorse? So I work for the predictable people and maybe I stay alive longer. I do keep my friends in the other groups. I have family scattered all around; no cab driver knows this city better. You want something, I know where to get it."

"I want to find a hostage."

"Any hostage in particular?"

"Yes."

"I doesn't matter. They're all in the same part of town. Dahya."

"Can you take me there? Not now. Tomorrow."

"I don't like to go there." He thought noisily and then said, "No, it's all right. I'll be your driver."

We passed another checkpoint, at the fabled Green Line. Regular Lebanese Armed Forces manned it, and there was a real booth with government insignia on it, but aside from that it was the same as the others: young boys with powerful toys, careless and threatening. I did not see whether Amir covered and uncovered his gun, but he seemed to know the boys with the guns. They waved us through into downtown, where the city became at once more cosmopolitan and pedestrian. Arabic replaced French and English in the store signs and posters, and the buildings and streets became more crowded, dirtier, older. I felt no threat, just the quease of uncertainty.

"Tell me something. When do I need to get in a cab to get home by dark?"

"This time of year? Nine, maybe nine-thirty."

"You meet me at nine in front of the Paris Hotel and on the way home we'll work a deal for you to drive me while I'm here."

"It's a deal already. We don't need another ride to settle it."

47.

Ten minutes after Amir let me go, I had no idea where I was. The signs of turmoil cropped up like mutants, a machine gun here, a shell-demolished building there, graffiti and posters of dark-eyed mullahs everywhere. But aside from the leery eyes the people of Beirut cast at anyone who draws near, the city limped along its business like any city suddenly reduced to half its population and a fraction of its glory. People drove by in expensive metal, guarded by boys in open jeeps. Carefully dressed women shopped in stores which never raised their grates from their windows. Something was wrong with Beirut, you could tell, but what was wrong was that it felt so strange without being all that different. I expected alien, alien I can deal with—you just let the natives lead. But people rushing in and out of cabs and buses, hurrying their bags and briefcases, all felt so common you could scream, until you realized they were hurrying because they might have just set a bomb somewhere, that the bags and briefcases might themselves be bombs about to be set, that the cabs and buses might be the next targets.

I walked away from the sun. Amir had left me off at the Paris Hotel, so we could agree where to meet later. "You don't know how important precision can be in Beirut," he told me. "Precision is the difference between sleeping in your own bed tonight or shivering chained to a cot." I explored the blocks around the hotel. A clot of LAF soldiers cadged a bottle from a bar and drank in an alley. Women wrapped head-to-toe in black stood silent as statues in the shadows of doorways. A man crouching against a wall cleaned his gun, looking at me as though he wished the gun was assembled and loaded. What in the world am I doing here? These people owe me nothing, no good will even. I don't know what they are fighting for and I don't care. I want to be home, eating pizza with Elizabeth, rubbing her feet after she's had a long day running around the world putting out, or setting, fires.

The sun directly overhead looked larger, more fierce. You could smell a lingering smoke when you passed some rubble, as though something foul had been burned. Even huge buildings, old buildings—still used, still occupied—bore signs of shell shock. On the corniche, the long swirl of sandy beach at the western edge of the city, stood a ten-storey hotel, windows and sometimes walls blown away, a dead hulk casting powerless eyes onto the Mediterranean.

"I understand you can still call their worldwide reservations number and reserve a room." A thin blond man in bathing suit, pale blue cover-up and red-framed glasses appeared beside me. "You're overdressed for the beach."

"I wasn't planning on coming here."

"That's just as well. Keep them guessing." His voice lilted, a light mixture of an English accent and gay affectation. "You must be new here."

"How can you tell?"

"You're being watched, but you have no guard."

I whipped my head around to look across the broad avenue that separates the beach walk from the rest of the city. A horde of innocuous-looking strangers drank simultaneously from demitasse cups at a café across the street.

"Third table from the left is my guess." I could only see

the legs of a man and fingers grasping a newspaper. "I wouldn't worry much about it. They just like to know who you are."

I held out my hand for a shake. "Ron Stutzer. From the US."

"Brian Bowman." He gave a limp shake. "I'm from here."

"Here?"

"East Beirut. My family has business interests in the Middle East."

"I'm staying up in the hills myself."

"With anyone? Or in an American safe-house?"

"How safe are those houses if everyone knows about them?"

"Safe enough, if you pay your duty. But it's very cramped up there. I like the beach much better."

"Even now?" I tried to guess his age. Twenty-two? Had the war gone on his whole life?

"It's actually a bit better now. A few years back every grain of sand was either mined or shelled. Of course that didn't stop the sun-worshippers. The army cleans up the body parts and two hours later the people come back. I once got kicked while I was diving into the water, but the foot wasn't attached to anyone. Must have been blown out to sea."

"I'm not sure I like this place."

"If gunpowder had never been invented, this place would be heaven. Liking Beirut only takes a little imagination." He chuckled. "A lot of imagination. Follow me."

I held back. I didn't know the man.

Brian turned back to me. "We're just going across the street to the café."

"But the man you say is following me is there."

"Right. So why make him work hard? We'll sit next to him. Remember, I'm not interested in your answer, but when I ask you what you're doing in Beirut, tell me you're traveling for pleasure." I followed him. "It gets them every time."

48.

The bar of the Paris looked like any hotel bar, except the backbar had no mirrors. I was a moment late, because I taken time to exchange addresses and phone numbers with Brian. Andrea sat in a corner, two empty glasses in front of her. She gulped the third as I joined her.

"The best gin-and-tonics. I don't know why. They always tasted like gunpowder to me before."

"Maybe that's why you like them."

"Maybe that's why I like them here."

"Wonderful city. I've never been in a war zone before."

Her bleached eyes wafted over to the bartender. When he looked her way she raised her glass again. "Today was a quiet day. No shelling at all, almost no shooting. Usually the smoke from the ordnance makes downtown dirtier than Los Angeles."

"I can't believe the people who go to the beach. I met someone there who said unexploded shells just litter the whole thing."

"Someone? Someone who?"

I thought: Whoa! is this girl jealous? But then I realized her honest concern about people I met by chance. It looks bad in Washington when an American civilian dies. That's why Elizabeth's capture provoked more sympathy than the General's supposed death. "Brian Bowman. He said he was a native, spoke with an English accent."

"A fag?" I nodded, but then shrugged. "He's harmless. At least to anyone but himself."

"He seemed to like taking risks."

A waiter in a starched but stained white vest brought a tray with three tall thin glasses filled with sparkle and a whole slice of lime. "Et pour monsieur?"

"Do you want one?" I tipped my head OK. "Rien pour monsieur," she said. "C'est tout."

"You speak French."

"One of the requirements for the job here. Even most of the people carrying guns speak French. They used to own this place." She drank. "What kinds of risks did he take?"

"Who?"

"Bowman."

I told her about sitting beside the man Brian thought tailed me. He ignored us completely, but I saw him later, on my way to meet Andrea. I supposed Brian was right.

"His family has deep ties on both sides of the line. His mother's father was a powerful Arab, his father's mother a Gamayel. He's immune so long as he doesn't interfere. He can tweak all the noses he wants to."

"Did I tweak the wrong nose, sitting with him?"

She shrugged, finished the first of her two drinks. When she put the glass down she held the slice of lime in her teeth. "Party trick," she said. "It depends. I think he was offering his protection. It might just be a seduction ploy. Did you find out anything today?"

"I found out the name of the neighborhood where she's being held."

"Dahya?"

"How did you know?"

"They're all held there. Well, not all, but most of them. It's a rabbit warren of rubble and tiny streets. The place is better watched than East Beirut, and they don't like Americans."

"If you know where Elizabeth is, why don't you go in and get her?"

"And get a dozen people killed? And cause an international incident? And jeopardize our other interests in the Middle East?" Andrea swallowed her other drink and waved the glass at the bartender again. Her eyes began to dribble out of focus. "It's not a simple problem, Ron. And there aren't any simple answers."

"Not for the government. I don't have the same goals, I guess."

"That's your right, when you're back home. Here you don't have that right. You should be careful who you tell what."

I wanted to say, What? will you assassinate me? I stopped myself, because I realized even before I spoke that she would. We fell silent. The head honcho brought us our drinks this time, my second, Andrea's sixth and seventh. He spoke with her in quiet French. I only understood one word, Hezbollah, which he said with a native's inflection. When he left, Andrea said, "Look at the bartender."

I wheeled in my seat. He was putting the bottles from the mirrorless backbar into crates and replacing them with others. "What is he doing?"

"What does it look like?" I knew the belligerent drinker's tone too well to answer her. She said, "The Muslim nationalists don't believe in alcohol, so every now and again they come and shoot up a bar."

"So?"

"Would you leave your expensive liquor out if you knew it was about to by shot to pieces?"

"They know?"

"Sure they know. They get a call from someone in Hezbollah who tells them. They're only trying to make a point, not escalate the war. They want to make some rules for a night: no drinking! So they call, tell the bar when, the bar tells us, and we leave right before they come. They shoot up the old bottles and then leave and then the bar closes for the night."

"You drink a lot, don't you?"

"Here, you bet. Have you ever cleaned up after a car bomb? You don't have to see two kids with a gearshift sticking out their bellies to want to drink a lot. Let's finish these up. We've only got ten more minutes. Less, if we want a good seat for the raid."

49.

"You are the man looking for the American girl?"

It was him, the man Brian and I had sat beside at the café by the beach. He wore an old American-cut suit and a bright red tie. His pudgy face almost swallowed his thin lips. I looked around for Andrea, but I couldn't spot her in the crowd trying not to mill too close to the entrance to the Paris Hotel bar.

"Elizabeth?" I asked, "You know where she is?"

"You cannot speed," he said. "I will negotiate with you, but you must bring one thousand dollars good-faith money."

"Where? When?"

"At the Café Corniche, at eleven in the morning. You will come alone?" he asked, but he did not wait for a reply.

50.

I think all the tutoring began to sink in, because I told neither Andrea nor Amir about the next day's meeting. For someone like me, who finds it so easy to doubt the value of my existence, it was easy to accept that the people who most often warned you to be discreet were the ones you most needed to be discreet around. If trust goes out the window, then the people trying the hardest to earn your trust must be the ones to trust least. I understood Hussein and his well-paid thugs—they found the best deal in town, a way to live well and stay safely behind those casually slung automatics. And I thought I understood the mysterious man, who not only tailed me but also presented himself as an emissary—they want money for Elizabeth.

But Andrea? Amir? What were they after? She's just an American doing her job, securing lives behind enemy lines. What, in a gin-and-tonic haze? I offered her a ride back home via Amir, but she said she had her own transportation and pointed at a coterie of LAF—Lebanese Armed Forces—jeeps called in to clean up the aftermath of the Hezbollah attack.

The attack itself? Like a movie set. Hotel people hastened patrons out of the bar and far from the the entrance. A van with no lights on and gun-slots chiseled out of the panels skidded to a halt in the middle of the full street which ran in front of the hotel. One older man wearing a black kaftan and a turban stepped from somewhere, the crowd I think, and began to direct the half a dozen gunmen. In a gunpowder fury, they shouted many things about Allah, funnelled into the bar and let off a quick round of ammunition. I never knew guns could make such a racket.

Then, two bearded men in what I took to be traditional garb came out and posted themselves on either side of the door. The mullah gave them a command, and these guys scared the skivvies off of the crowd by firing a quick burst not far enough above our heads. A number of people crumbled to the pavement, certain they were hit; I crouched myself. The remainder of the hit squad charged out of the bar and into the van. It took off with the two guards who fired at the sky hanging on to the open doors in the back.

I found Andrea leaning against the hotel awning support. "Are they all like this?" I asked.

She shrugged. "Every now and again they get sloppy, go to the wrong bar, destroy some real liquor. Sometimes the LAF or the Syrians decide they won't put up with the disorder and a gunfight cames down. Sometimes bystanders buy it, but not often. Bad word-of-mouth from that. It's all show."

As she was talking I watched the mullah walk away across the street, a handful of faithful in tow. "What about him? Isn't someone going to stop him?"

"For what? Blessing his flock?"

I could see where I would get with Andrea. She was numb. She had no outrage to give. "Does this close the bar?" was all I could ask.

"For tonight. They have to clean up, get the alcohol out from the back."

"Are they really so determined to be dry? The Muslims, I mean."

"I grew up in the south," Andrea told me, "and our religious fervor is like a popgun to their whole arsenal. One on one? Maybe some of them drink. Get them in power you won't live fifteen minutes smelling of alcohol."

"So you'll be back here tomorrow?"

"Should be safe for a few months now," she nodded. "Call me during the day just to check in."

Amir met me as promised and we set the terms for him driving me. I asked him about Brian Bowman, and he offered to get me a list of all the people he'd slept with in the past two years. I figured that was proof enough of his knowledge of the town. "Where does Bowman live?" I asked.

"At the top of your hill." Surprise crept into his voice, surprise at my innocence is my only guess. "Hussein's their man. Bowman gets a slice of the money you pay for protection."

51.

Getting money from the bank proved easier than I could have hoped. Ignoring the guards and guns, the bank felt remarkably like the main branch of any bank, with grey-haired, grey-suited men seated behind a swarm of desks, defending the bastions of cash. Once I made my business clear, my grey man ushered me into the company of another more important one. He had a bigger desk and, I gathered, more cash to defend. I asked for $5,000, still enough money for me to gasp and choke on, and my banker asked, "American? In what denominations?"

I eyed the street outside the bank like a secret service agent, those men who announce their secret missions with every glance at the crowd around them. Encouraged by the peace the day before, people thronged to the street, shops opened wide. The city roused itself in respite from fear.

The sun cooperated with the celebratory ambience. The Eastern hills keep Beirut cool later in the morning than you might think. By ten, Amir dismissed until noon and the bank errand handled, the sun rose to meet a shade of fleecy clouds. Temperature wouldn't hit ninety until afternoon, if at all. People smiled everywhere; good weather always produces good tempers, even in intemperate places.

I found my man at the Café Corniche with no hesitation. He seemed as alone as I did, but I could guess that at least one of the other tables hosted a gun-toting companion. "Welcome and good morning, Mr. Stutzer!" My man gestured me to the only other chair at his table. "I am very glad you have come to talk with me."

He did not offer his hand for a shake. I suspect he regarded me as Christian vermin and preferred not to touch me. "You have an advantage over me. I don't know your name."

"Call me Ahmet Avai. It is not the only advantage I have over you."

"You have my friend."

He held up his hand. "Please, we must drink before we talk. Some coffee? I must have a sweet. My teeth are very sweet."

Avai arranged for some coffee, thick sweet stuff you can drink only the smallest taste of. If you sip too deep into the cup the grounds will gag you. His honey cake smelled less overwhelming than the coffee.

Avai had seated me with my back to the sea, so I turned in my chair to get a glimpse of the morning sun on the water. Near where I had met him yesterday, Brian stepped out of a small Mercedes limousine. He saw me immediately, and I had to shake him off to prevent his coming over.

Avai noticed. "It can pay to have powerful friends, but only if they are friends first and powerful after."

"We're neighbors. Neighbors often have more common interests than friends."

"Mr. Bowman is a foolish young man, and not always the best of friends."

"I have your thousand dollars. I see this as a retainer. It

entitles me to your good faith, just as my bringing it proves mine."

"Perhaps. Do not present it to me now. Leave it on the table when you go." I nodded. "We must proceed in small steps. I do not know you. You do not know me. Each step we will need to prove faith. I work with many people. You demonstrate faith to me. This does not demonstrate faith to them."

"You have my friend?"

"You want to gallop. We must crawl."

"I see no point in crawling with you if you do not have what I want."

"Then you must gallop without me. Remember that it makes no difference how fast you go if you only travel in a circle."

"Then what is the next step?"

"You must meet with my friends."

"I will meet with your friends if they bring proof that they have my friend and that she's fine."

"Will a videotape satisfy you?"

"Yes. Sure."

"Such videotapes are very expensive in Beirut. Your thousand dollars has bought only today's meeting."

"How much for the videotape?"

"Twenty-five thousand dollars."

I thought, Yikes! and then, They could sell me a blank tape. "That's a fair price only after I have seen the video."

"That is something you will have to negotiate with my friends. I have only this to bring you: you must meet us in Dahya. Do you know where is the southern checkpoint to Dahya?"

"My driver does."

"Your driver, Amir, is a snake. But the only dangerous snakes are the ones who hide. He will bring you."

"I cannot meet you in Dahya. I have no way of knowing I will get out."

"Very true."

"I have shown myself willing to meet with you. I will bring the money, I will meet you any time you want, but I can't offer myself as your hostage. That gets me nothing."

He looked ready to argue, but then thought better of it. "If you will allow me, I will speak now to my friends to grant this point." He nearly bolted from the table and into the darkness of the café kitchen. I searched the walk across the way for Brian, but I could not see him. Before I was certain Avai could find a phone he was back. "We will meet you outside the northern checkpoint of Dahya. There is a petrol pump a hundred meters before, on the right. Behind the building there you will find a small field. There we will meet."

"When?"

"Why tonight, of course. No later than ten. We cannot guarantee your safety past eleven."

I pulled the envelope with the $1,000 from my pocket. "I hope this will cover the tab, Mr. Avai."

"Yes, yes." He smiled and put his hand on the envelope. I crossed over to the beach.

52.

"They won't kill you," Brian told me, kicking his heels into the rocky sand. "That's not a promise that they will deal honestly with you."

"Is this stupid? Should I just bag it?"

"Your American slip is showing!" He ran his hand through his hair. "I'm thinking of dyeing it jet-black, with some bleached white at the temples. What do you think?"

"What do you mean?"

"Americans have always made the mistake in the Middle East—maybe it's just as true elsewhere—of equating civilized with American. If the enemy does not deal on American terms, you go in with guns. But now the Islamic Jihad has the guns and they want to deal on their terms."

"So it's hopeless."

"Maybe. But the Arab way is to acknowledge it may be hopeless—and keep negotiating until it is. They may regard the whole thing as hopeless, but they don't want to tell you that yet. They may not know what they want. They may want to make you crawl before they negotiate."

"It's hopeless." I worried about the $1,000 I left for Avai. I asked Brian if he knew the man.

He laughed.

"When the Israelis came in 1982, they kicked out the PLO but left the Syrians to take over. The Iranian Ambassador to Damascus hired a man named Avai to co-ordinate attacks here. No one knows who the man really was, but even before he disappeared terrorists went by that name in negotiations. Avai is the spirit of Allah; he is everywhere."

I watched the Mediterranean lap a thousand miles from the Atlantic. "Do I go through with this?"

"What choice do you have?"

"I can wait for another break, something with a little more promise. These people might not even have Elizabeth. I give them twenty-five thousand dollars to prove nothing?"

"You give them the money to prove you want your friend back. They know her father is rich. They don't know how deep he will allow their hands in his pockets. You agreed to twenty-five thousand dollars without blanching. They will think the money has no end."

"I misplayed it?"

"Maybe. They might not have shown themselves willing to negotiate at all if you asked to cut them off at ten thousand dollars. They know there is a balance between

time in captivity and money, but they don't know where
your balance point is. You know—or maybe you don't—
that there's a balance between the value she has as a hostage
and the value the dollars have in their pockets, but you
don't know how many dollars it will take to tip the scale.
So you go, lose twenty-five thousand dollars if you are
wrong, invest it if you are right."

"How did you learn this?"

"I grew up here. Just remember, my protection will stop
them from killing you, and most likely from taking you
hostage. It will not stop them from crossing you."

53.

Amir drove south in the waning light. The daytime
youths at the checkpoints looked older and more hostile in
the dusk. I had gotten used to being asked for my passport
at gunpoint, now; I had not gotten used to how small the
bore of an automatic weapon really was, or how big it
looked, or how small a hole it took for life to escape a
human body: bigger than a bee sting, but not much.

Amir had his doubts about this whole journey. "They
will kill you and then they will kill me."

"Is that worse than their killing you first and then me?"

"That's not an answer. I don't want to go at all. At
night? Into Dahya? With an American? I must be crazy!"

But still he drove. "You tell me how much money it will
cost to get you to do it."

"You Americans! Always a matter of money!"

"How much?"

He drove ahead in silence. We passed a Syrian checkpoint, a very easygoing operation; the guns muzzles stayed outside the car. "If we get out of this alive," Amir finally said, "then I will set my price."

"And if we don't?"

He smiled, I saw in the rearview mirror. We sat back-and-front on Amir's insistence. It made us look less like conspirators and made him less likely to be hit by bullets aimed at me. "Then I will make Hell very unpleasant for you."

The scene looked just as Avai described it, the checkpoint—marked by a small fire and the dull glint of steel—in eyesight beyond the closed gas station. There were no lights. The gas station seemed not to have been used for years, though in Beirut, where two-thousand-year old hovels served as storefronts and new hotels for shell practice, any use was possible. The pumps, glass broken or perhaps shot out of their faces, hugged the wall like the witnesses to the Paris Hotel shooting.

Amir slowed down as soon as he saw the flame of the checkpoint a quarter of a mile ahead. "Now that we are here, we should decide how we will do this."

"You have nothing to do but keep the car running and not leave me here."

"I will leave both doors open and stand beside the car with my hands up, so they will see I am not armed."

"I hope it won't matter."

"In such foolishness, every little thing matters."

I did not expect Avai, somehow. He had seemed like just a functionary. But there he stood, a solid ghost in Amir's dim sweeping headlights. Perhaps his function wasn't over. Perhaps only he spoke English. Perhaps he worked alone, scamming Western liberators. Amir stopped the car ten yards from the man, solitary in the dark, flashlight in hand. The field, as far as I could tell, was a packed-dirt lot with a handful of ruined cars. Other victims? I stepped out.

"Mr. Avai."

"Welcome, welcome, Mr. Stutzer. You will not mind walking toward me slowly with your hands ahead of you?" I took half a dozen steps. Now Avai said something in Arabic and Amir stepped out of the car and into the headlights, hands raised. He did leave the car doors open, at least.

"Thank you, Mr. Stutzer."

"I have your money, Mr. Avai. Do you have the tape?"

"Still impatient, Mr. Stutzer! Please greet my associates!" Three young men in traditional garb emerged from the shadows around the junked cars. They all carried those square, frightening weapons. I heard Amir murmur behind me. "Do not worry of the guns, please. They only illustrate our position."

"It would be easier not to worry if I knew the weapons were not loaded."

Avai chuckled in the dark. "Yes, but not knowing is perfectly your position."

"What now?"

"Follow the light of my torch if you please. Stay walking in the circle." He aimed the light at my feet and reeled me toward him. I felt the envelope of money—surprising how little space $25,000 can take—bobble against my side in the pocket of my light jacket. Two arms-lengths from him he stopped me. "Please stand to there," Avai said to me and then he said something quickly and gruffly to his three youths. They surrounded me and patted me down. Without a fumble they took the cash and handed it to Avai. He put his flashlight under his arm and ran his thick fingers through the cash, not so much counting as weighing the dollars.

"You are a most co-operative negotiator, Mr. Stutzer. You have kept your bargain." He reached behind him, under his coat inside his belt. I expected a gun and a quick flash, but there in his hand was a videotape. Waving the envelope at me, he said, "At our table, you must pay before the roll of the dice." He barked something to his boys.

One of them swung his gun and hit me hard just below my right knee. That was the one I hurt the most my years on the football field. I crumbled to the dirt. Before I could respond I saw two guns pointed at my face. The darkness around me was daylight compared to the fathomless dark of those gun barrels. I was on my left side, both hands holding my right calf, where they hit me.

Avai stepped up close to me and dropped the tape under my chin. He shone his light into my eyes. I could see nothing else.

"You will find there what we want next of you. May Allah preserve you." He clicked off his light and disappeared. The flashes in my eyes didn't stop me from feeling what happened next. A cold gun barrel lay flat along the back of my neck and then exploded into the dirt behind my right ear. The world went blue, then red, then grey. I could not breathe. Then the world fell into a gun barrel, black all around.

54.

The pain brought me to. At first I felt I was in the nurse's office at my elementary school being poked searingly on my back because I had welts there. I don't ever remember remembering that before. They were welts my father raised with the leather tip of a cloth belt. "How did this happen?" the nurse asked. Her name drifts away from me now, but I remember she smelled like the powder that came in the plastic pink cylinder my grandmother kept on her dresser.

"I don't remember." That became my motto for pain. Frustrated the hell out of my trainers later. They always wanted to know how you hurt yourself. "I don't remember." And I didn't remember anything about being hit by my father when I was a boy. A moment after I grasp the memory of that nurse's office, it closes off again into darkness and I open my eyes.

I'm at the barracks where Andrea first took me, where I spent my first night in Beirut. American institutions are painted the same color everywhere in the world. I lay on my right side. My neck felt on fire. Voices mumbled like the hum of bees in the cold, punctuated with a small sharp ping. My left ear rang with a panicky shrillness and felt ragged, as though I'd forced my head through a space too narrow for it. Andrea lowered her face to my line of sight and then stood up again. I thought I heard her voice somewhere. Seeing her did not surprise me. My pain did.

A man in a white coat came from behind me and put his face near mine. He was Arab. It sounded like he said, "You will be all right."

People have heard that so many times it lacks any power to reassure. I started to say something, but a huge ache welled up at the back of my jaw. The ache set up a chain reaction of pain: jaw, ear, neck on fire.

Some kind of gel slipped on my neck and eased the fire. I smelled the rubbing alcohol before I felt the cool sting on my ear, the warming trickle down my face and the front of my neck.

I think I faded out again. The next I remember, I lay on my back propped up on pillows. The side of my head, from just in front of and above my ear to the base of my neck, cowered under a bandage. I saw Andrea and the Arab doctor sitting in the two bent-chrome chairs by the door and an American soldier standing at arms behind them.

He was not nearly as reassuring as you might think.

I tried to speak out, but the ache flooded back. Did I break my jaw? No, it moved, but hurt like hell when it did. I spoke with it still instead.

"Where is Amir?"

Both Andrea and the doctor broke from their conversation and came over to me, Andrea to the right and the doctor standing to my left. He prodded the edges of the bandage and shone a small penlight in my eyes. Like Avai. No one said a thing. I repeated my question; maybe I mumbled more than I thought. "Where is Amir?"

Andrea said, "Your driver?" I tried to nod, but my neck burned. "He filled us in on what happened, and we sent him home. Some of Commander Faid's men will take you home when the doctor says you can go." She pointed her chin at the Arab. He said something. I couldn't hear it.

"What did he say?"

"He says you'll be all right."

His mouth moved again, and I thought I caught some words. "I can't hear what he's saying. The bandage."

"He can't hear you on that side." Andrea went to the soldier at the door, who stepped out. The doctor took Andrea's place by my other side.

"You have received quite a trauma, Ron Stutzer," the doctor said. He had slicked his thin hair close to his skull and spoke with an odd accent which sounded almost French. "The gun shot directly into the ground behind your head. This scattered the pebbles and dirt against your neck and ear. I have removed as much of this as I could see. We will have to wait a day for the healing to push out what I could not find."

"My jaw." Andrea came to the foot of the bed.

"We thought you might have broken it for a while," she said, her voice sounding like a neighbor's in a thin-walled apartment building. "But the doctor says it's just bruised."

"Yes, back here, on the other side." His finger touched the corner of the jaw just below my right ear. I tensed for pain, but none came. A gentle touch. "I believe that a large rock kicked up by the bullet struck you there. I felt no chips or fragments, but you will need an X-ray in confirmation."

"We can get you one tomorrow." Andrea's voice again sounded distant.

"My ear?"

"There will be some scarring. Cartilage always heals slowly, so it will be a month, maybe more, before you know what will become of the ear. You might desire reconstructive surgery."

I said again what I meant before. "My hearing."

"Ah." Andrea perched herself on the foot of the bed, careful not to rock me. "This we cannot yet say. The bang of a gun comes when the bullet comes out of the barrel, just at that point. So your ear was very close to the bang. I looked to see if there was trauma to the eardrum, puncture or what have you, but I could find none. That does not mean we can be sure. You will need a more careful examination."

"So I'm deaf."

Andrea put her hand on my ankle, for comfort.

"I would not say so. It could be that you have only a temporary deafness from the loudness of the noise. It could be the loud noise caused permanent loss of only part of your hearing, and in the next week you will get it back up to that point. That is, unless there is some actual damage to the ear I did not find." The doctor cleared his throat. "The good news is that the worst of your pain will heal the soonest. You received a burn across your neck. These people must have held the gun against you for ten seconds after they pulled the trigger. The burn is slight, but painful. I have ordered some pain relievers for you."

"What should I do now?"

"Medically? Stay off your feet for two days, recover from the trauma, and then go someplace fine for treatment. But I do not know that you will have that chance."

Colonel Harbison came in then, followed by the soldier Andrea had sent to fetch him. Andrea stepped away saluting, and Harbison came to the foot of the bed. "I see our neighborhood terrorists gave you a welcome party." I said nothing. The doctor shrank back; clearly the patient had been taken from his hands. "That was one very stupid maneuver, Stutzer. I thought you knew there was no dealing with these people."

"Not your way, maybe," I mumbled.

"What did you say, Stutzer?"

Andrea said, "He's been injured, sir. He's speaking as clearly as he's able."

"So what did he say, Captain?"

Andrea hesitated. " 'Maybe not your way, sir.' "

"The local Arab population has declared war, Stutzer. We have not. I wish we had, then I could evacuate you. I've talked with the Ambassador about your case. While he's mulling over what to do, I recommend you stay close to home. I don't want to hear you've been trying to buy a hostage with twenty-five thousand dollars."

"The tape."

"We're taking care of that," Harbison spat. "I'd like to see you and the doctor in my office after he's been taken home," he said to Andrea on his way out.

"Yes, sir," she said to the closing door.

"Where's the tape?"

"Your driver left it when he dragged you to the cab and brought you here. He had no idea how badly you were hurt."

"Did you go get it? It might be where he left it."

"It was. People are looking at it right now." She looked at the doctor. "It doesn't look like much. The first few minutes were pornography."

"Pornography?" Suddenly I couldn't breathe. I thought of Elizabeth, forced into a sexual performance. "What do you mean, pornography?"

"Porn. They use those tapes sometimes. The Arabs love

American pornography, but the Hezbollah regards it as a crime. They confiscate the tapes and record over them, but they usually bury their message in the middle somewhere. They think it makes us look bad. It does, too."

"So, nothing but porn?"

"Not that I know. I haven't checked. The record tab hole has been taped over, so there's hope. They messed up the tape a little with their shot into the ground. Lots of dust."

"Could you find out?"

She hesitated. "Sure, if you do something for me."

"What?"

"Hussein's people will take you home. When you get there, get some sleep. I'll come in the morning with whatever news I have."

The doctor handed me a pill and some water. I took it.

55.

This time Andrea woke me with the doorbell before coming in on her own. She called my name. I was refereeing a struggle between my pain and my robe when she found me in the bedroom.

"I had to let myself in because I don't have a lot of time. Sorry."

"It's OK." My head was logy, whether from the pain or the medication I couldn't say. Even my left shoulder ached a bit this morning.

"I could get in big trouble telling you this. Harbison said he doesn't want you to know."

"Know what?" I tied my robe as though I really cared about it.

"Is there anything here to eat? I'm starving."

"Nothing." I had eaten next to nothing since I had arrived in Lebanon and felt starved too. "What? The tape?"

Andrea gave a quick nod, looking around. "Yeah. A half an hour into the porno there's thirty seconds of your friend sleeping and them waking her up. The guy who wakes her has his back to the camera. He tells her in Arabic to say she's all right. She says, 'I'm fine,' and then the porno comes back on."

"That's it? There isn't more?"

"Did they tell you there would be a message on it?"

"Yeah. I think so."

"A man named Hussein Moussavi, who runs Islamic Amal, one of the militias backed to the hilt by Iran, appears briefly on the tape ten minutes later. He says they will never negotiate your friend's release, except in exchange for prisoners in Israel. They know your friend's family has business interests there."

"Does he mean it?"

"There's no way to know. We're checking out whether that bit from Moussavi was dropped in from something else. We don't think he's in Beirut right now." We said nothing for a breath and then she said, "You can't tell anyone you know any of this. Call Harbison in an hour and ask him about the tape. Use whatever he tells you as your story. You're fighting a war in his trenches and he doesn't like it, so watch yourself."

"Whose side is he on?"

"The military's. He runs an intelligence/counter-terrorist outfit. Secret even at the Pentagon, as far as I can see. State and the CIA see him as a dangerous amateur, which is how he sees you. He wants to prove they're wrong about him. He might have to show you up to do it."

"So what should I do?"

"Leave?" My face showed my shock. "No, I know you won't. Just rest and watch your back very carefully, that's all."

"I can hardly turn my neck. I'll be lucky to cover my sides."

"Remember to call Harbison." She went for the door. "I need the protection."

56.

After Andrea left, I called Brian, the doctor, Amir and Harbison. The weather cooperated again. The cloud cover meant Brian would stay close to home. He seemed pleased to hear from me and invited me over.

"My God!" he exclaimed when his houseboy ushered me back to the sunny patio where he sat. "What did they do to you?"

"The doctor's still not certain."

"No permanent damage, I hope."

I gave my first laugh since I'd been shot. It came off thin. "The doctor's still not certain."

"Did you at least get something for your trouble?"

"The videotape."

"What did it say? Was your friend on it?"

"I don't know. I haven't seen it."

"Did you lose it somehow? What happened?"

"My driver left it at the drop when he dragged me to the car. He drove me to the American compound. They questioned him and went after the tape themselves."

"They found it?"

"Could I have some tea?"

"Certainly." Brian gestured to his servant, who wore a white tunic and royal blue pants. Brian wore white pants, even cleaner than the servant's tunic, and a royal blue shirt of polished cotton. His feet were encased in worn and neutral espadrilles.

"You haven't changed your hair yet."

"I have an appointment later today, and stop changing the subject. Didn't anyone tell you what the tape said?"

"Colonel Harbison did."

"The people in the hill call him the Mule, you know. He's stubborn, but you don't want to be behind him when he kicks."

"He told me the tape was a fake, nothing. Just a piece of badly made American pornography."

"Pornography? Oh yes, Hezbollah doesn't approve."

"So I gathered."

Brian studied his tea leaves a second, and then looked me in the eye. "Do you believe the Colonel?"

My laugh came out rounder this time. "No. Should I?" He shrugged and sat back, face turned to the sun, eyes closed. A bee scouted his forehead and then turned away. "Do you have bees, Brian?"

"What?"

"Bees. Do you keep bees?"

"The family has a few hundred hives, yes. Frankly, they frighten me. Are you an apiarist?"

"On a small scale, a couple dozen hives maybe. Not a commercial operation." The bee which rejected Brian's forehead discovered the honeypot on the table. "That one just found a gold mine."

"Probably wondering where he is; that could well be from his hive. Time was we exported honey. Not nearly as profitable as other things now."

I watched the bee fill herself up and fly off contentedly. You can almost see the smile a bee has when she's full of honey. A half an hour and a horde of her hive-mates would be back to suck up their own dram of the stuff. "You don't believe Harbison either."

He shrugged again. "Not for me to say, really."

"But?"

"But no, I don't."

"Why?"

"Think about it. Arabs love American pornography, unless they are born-again Muslims, in which case they loathe it just as passionately. If your Avai is not Hezbollah, he wouldn't give up his pornography when he could easily find some other tape or give you nothing at all. If he is Hezbollah . . .—Did he say the tape contained anything when he gave it to you?"

"That it would tell me what to do next."

"Did you tell Harbison that?"

"Sure."

"And he said?"

"He said, 'Just their way of telling you to fuck yourself.' Possible, isn't it?"

"No. 'Fuck' doesn't translate that way. In Arabic, it's always transitive, never reflexive. Fucking is always something you do to something else, for your pleasure."

"So, if Avai is Hezbollah?"

"Then he at least knows where your friend is, or knows who knows. Then you are either someone he can keep bilking or a real trader. If he just wants to bilk you, he doesn't hurt you. My guess is he has her and wants to deal. I lay you five to one Harbison is lying."

"So what should I do?"

"What does Harbison want you to do?"

"Go home."

"So you stay. Go to Dahya during the daytime. Let yourself be seen. If they didn't kill you last night they won't kill you now."

"You told me yesterday they wouldn't kill me last night."

"Well, did they? Did they even try?"

57.

After a long afternoon hospital trip with surprisingly little bad news, I went back to my prison-home for an exhausted twelve-hour sleep. I had two dreams I remember, both with bees. Not that strange for me really; bees often fly around my dreams. Sometimes the people in my dreams have wings, bee-wings, not angel-wings. With the shutters closed, my room became dark and close as a hive. I half dreamed and half remembered a hive Jim and I had up until two seasons back, before I met Elizabeth. We called it LP, because the bees were so temperamental they used to have thirty-three-and-a-third revolutions a minute, worse even than Langley. If the queen slackened her laying, they would raise another. If the new queen came back from her nuptial flight with only a half-full sac of semen, they struck her down and began grooming another princess. They had no mercy for majesty, like most bees, no reverence for royalty.

Once, they killed a new queen right after she had killed all of her possible successors. A hive without a queen falls to shameful, sad practices. One of the workers will inevitably take to laying eggs, but because she can't fertilize them, the eggs all grow up into drones. That's the great irony in bee biology: fathers have no fathers. All the eggs laid by a bee without sperm will grow into drones. So, in no time at all, LP looked like a hunting cottage, all fat boys scarfing up the honey and leaving droppings everywhere. Moths moved in, birds picked off the unmotivated bees who still went out to the fields, resigned. The beautiful excitement of LP crashed into a foul and smelly mess, because the hive killed their queen in a fit of fear or pique or addiction to drama.

It took me a whole day to clean the hive out and another to prepare it for a new community of bees. Even after we moved it off into an orchard alone, the hive has never been able to maintain a population of more than 30,000. The winter before last nearly killed it off completely. They limp along, forlornly, perhaps finding signs everywhere of the great battles that had been fought there, and this gruesome history overwhelms hope of any future accomplishment.

The second was dream pure and simple, not mixed up with memory. I was in a room or a hive flooded with bees. I might not have been in a room, but only in a winter ball. When the weather turns cold, bees gather into a ball and hang on tight to the bee beside them with the little hooks they all have on their feet. By squeezing together they raise the temperature at the middle, where they keep the queen. Always the ones at the middle push their way to the outside to eat and relieve themselves, and the ones on the outside push their way in for the warmth.

I was in the pulsing mass, not a victim, not a queen, just one of the bees in the heating ball, hanging onto the hooks of one neighbor and then another on my trip to the outside.

At the surface there were people flying in bee dances. Bees have a remarkable system of communication. They fly around the hive in circles when food is very near, as though they are saying, "Just go and look for it! You can't *help* but find it!" If the food's farther than a hundred yards away at most, they fly in figure eights. The line between the two circles of the eights shows the direction of the food. The speed with which they do these eights tells you how far. The swagger they show in the dance tells you how good the food there is.

Hooked onto the outside of the ball, dozens of bee-people hurl wild stories at me, masses of indecipherable information. People I know—Bienenkorb, Bea, my father, Jim, Andrea—and people I don't all fly patterns. I shout at them, "What do you know?!?" But they just fly and fly and buzz louder.

I peel off the bee-ball and walk away, out toward the light. When I look back, the ball looks just like a brain, floating in the dark.

The light of morning surprised me. I hobbled up and called Amir.

58.

The international calling center loomed like an armory, but had been mercifully untouched in the war. It seems even people in the passion of war prefer to destroy their past rather than jeopardize their future.

"This is Ron Stutzer in Beirut. I'd like to speak with Noah Jacobs."

A moment later he came on.

"Ron! Do you want us to come get you?"

"No, no. I'm just reporting in."

Even across the scratchy lines I heard a change of tone.

"Everything is all right, then?"

"More or less. Nothing out of control yet."

"Good, good. Have you found Betsy? I talk to her father every day and he wants to know."

"I'm on her trail."

"Will you need more money? The man is willing to go one mill for release, but that will leave you short for expenses."

"I might. I'll know better soon." I'm used to cradling the phone on my left ear. In the midst of overwhelming strangeness, the little discomfort nagged. My left ear throbbed. "Tell him that everything seems to be going well."

"You're not in any danger, are you Ron? There's no point in losing two trying to save one."

"They seem more concerned with killing each other than killing me."

His voice hitched. "That's something to be thankful for. We can be there in an hour, if you need us. You sure you're all right?"

I wanted to ask, Have you heard I'm not? but I didn't want the answer. Better to know that I just couldn't know. I said, "I'm in my element. I never felt so much at home in my life."

The plastic mouthpiece smelled like old coffee and the wooden booth like ammonia. My jaw hurt more from this bout of lying than from the longer conversation in the morning with Brian. Of course, I denied myself pain pills; I wanted to be alert this afternoon.

"Still a sense of humor," Jacobs echoed. "We got you down for a week from now."

"You might want to be ready sooner. Is the professor there?"

"Nusanti? No, we sent him back home. Classes or something. Got a question for him?"

"Nothing I can put into words."

A pause grew into a hollow, and he filled it. "Only an hour away, Ron. Remember."

I arced the receiver back to its hook and stayed in the booth a moment, staring at the phone. How many people listened to that conversation? How many thought they knew what it was about, or what it meant?

59.

"One trip to Dahya was not enough for you? You want
to be shot again? You want me shot?"

I had just stepped out of the bank, where I had arranged
to withdraw $200,000 in cash. Naturally, they did not have
the dollars on hand; they would get them packeted in the
next day, however they do it in this sorry place. Downtown had a creepy, eerie smell that afternoon. Three car
bombs had blown in succession, and an old building collapsed in the rumble. A fire started, and whatever had been
inside the building left a yellow miasma as it smoldered
into the midday siesta.

"It's better than staying here."

"OK, but what's wrong with the hills? What's wrong
with the country club? We have to go to Dahya for you to
enjoy yourself?"

I handed him a bundle of the Grumbler's hundreds. "A
thousand. For last night and today."

He flopped them in his hand twice and then put them
under his cap. "A thousand dollars makes it better. But
don't think it solves anything."

"Just drive, Amir. Back to the same gate. Find a café on
a busy street."

"You want coffee? I know a good café on the corniche.
We go to Dahya for coffee?"

"Just drive."

I amazed myself with my complacency at the guns we
faced at the checkpoints riding down there. But my own
amazement just didn't compare to the obvious shock and
wonder on the faces of the Amal guards at the south Dahya
checkpoint. They barked "Bezbat! Bezbat!" in the window
before they took a look in the car. Three sets of eyes wid-

ened at once. I thought I recognized the face of one of Tuesday's gunmen among the guards. They fell back from the car and argued among themselves for a breath of time—and then waved us through.

"Why look at the passport of a ghost?" Amir said. "You will be dead soon enough. They can examine your passport all they want then."

"They're going to Avai now. We don't have a lot of time for surprise. Get us to the most central cafe in this part of Dahya."

"It's Sheik Abdul's, just off the square. But that's where the Amal goes."

"How far?"

"Fifty meters. A hundred."

"Then park it."

"Here? I want to keep my eye on it."

"I'll buy you a new one if anyone touches it."

"I will drive it in heaven if they turn it into a bomb."

I couldn't have asked for a better reaction when I stepped out of the car. A twelve-year-old kid squinted across the street at me and then looked behind him. In a flash, he disappeared in a filthy alley between buildings. A mullah scowled and made a point of looking away from where the boy had gone, though he hadn't seen him.

"What are we doing?" Amir whined.

"We're going for coffee," I told him, "and we're keeping our eyes open."

"My eyes will do you no good. I'm blind with fear."

In the square again I witnessed the dances. Most people could not grasp my presence. Their faces, their postures even, went blank. But some hopped on one foot, and others turned circles. Their eyes kept bouncing off where the first boy had run. Their faces became maps of fear, of panic, of alertness. No one threatened us, no one even gestured. My white bandage broadcast my status as alien, intruder, enemy, even more than my skin and dress. I stood tall as I could, my sleeves rolled up to show my thick white arms. I could gain nothing by hiding now. They were the ones hiding something, and they would tell me where it, she, was. Elizabeth.

Sheik Abdul's was the first doorway on the first alley to the right off the square. I called the angle the eyes shot to noon; with the big mosque in the square as the hub, Abdul's was at about nine o'clock. Tables crowded the street, leaving just enough room for a man and mule to pass without feeling as though the animal had just stepped on your lunch. I grabbed a table up front. The other patrons watched us unabashedly. Two left, going each way up the alley, but most stayed and watched, talked among themselves and gestured. I saw three elbows jerk back, toward a little shy of noon.

Not far off that main street, then.

"We should go. They will not serve us here."

"You're wrong. Look." A bedraggled, bearded man and a husky clean-shaven one stared and gestured at me. The bearded one waved the back of his hand toward us, and then turned away from Abdul. It could only mean he'd been ordered to serve us.

He came to our table, saying nothing, signifying nothing. "What now?" Amir asked.

"Order for us. Can't you see he's waiting?" I bowed my head to Abdul, smiling. The pain in my neck brought a wince to my jaw, an echo of sympathetic pain.

Amir ordered. "The specialty. Word on the street says it's good, but I don't know what it is." People on the street pass news of pastry and hostages. No one ever keeps a secret. Nothing changes people like knowledge does. Confusion isn't having two pieces of contradictory knowledge, it's having them in the same place at the same time.

The specialty was exquisite, a flourless almond cake flooded with honey. From the taste of the honey I would have said it came from Brian's family apiaries, a poorer version of what he served me. It could be, too, that all honey tastes the same in this land, very sweet and curiously dry.

We were on our second coffee when Avai came. He was surrounded by guards, who took up positions ten yards off in either direction. He looked more out of place in his native clothing than he did in western rags.

"Good afternoon, Mr. Avai."

"Mr. Stutzer." He said nothing to Amir and acknowledged him only fractionally. "I hope that the warning shot did not make you stupid, Mr. Stutzer."

"Deaf, perhaps, but not stupid."

"Then I must compliment you of being brave."

" 'On being brave'." He nodded acceptance of the correction. "I wanted to thank you in person for the tape." I kept my hands on the table. One of Avai's guards had a gun pointed at me, I felt certain.

"You would have had that opportunity without coming in Dahya." Abdul brought Avai a coffee and specialty; he did not need asking. "Would you like more coffee?" I nodded and he ordered for me. Amir did not exist to him.

"I have not had the luxury of viewing the tape, Mr. Avai. I understand you have my friend."

"Do you also understand that we do not see the need to negotiate?"

"Of course."

"Then before you make an offer which will embarrass both of us, I have the authority to open a discussion with five million dollars."

My coffee came and I sipped it. The hot sweetness, the rush at the back of my head, brought a deep, soothing breath. I did not want to have to get used to this coffee, but I could, I could.

"Does my willingness to work from that figure earn my friend some comfort?"

"Your friend has received no harm. She is fed, she is warm."

"How about a gift."

"A gift? She has no use of perfumes and chocolates, Mr. Stutzer. We have no interest in any sort of tricks. A gift!"

"It will comfort her. She can't be an easy hostage. This might help."

"What gift do you have in mind?"

"Bees, Mr. Avai."

"Honeybees?"

"Just some queens and attendants. Small cages. No place to hide anything."

"Honeybees?"

"A private pleasure for her."

"And in exchange for your friend's comfort with these honeybees you will call your sources for more money. You see that we know what are your limits."

"I will call tomorrow morning, from the central telephone office. And the bees?"

"Let us meet here in two days. Sabbath—a time of peace. If these honeybees are as you say to me, I will see that she gets them. Then we will talk of her release."

"Thank you."

He bowed. "It is an honor to share a table with a brave man, Mr. Stutzer. My guard will see you and your driver to the checkpoint."

60.

"Bees!" Amir cried, once we were well beyond the checkpoint. "I see you are a lunatic. Brave? Hah! Brave as a boil! A lunatic has more sense than to try to be this brave!"

"Amir," I asked, once we passed the next checkpoint, more boys regarding their weapons just as I now did, "do you know anything about bees?"

"They make honey! They sting! What else is there to know?"

"Nothing. Elizabeth likes them, that's all." I stared out the window at the ragged housing. Amir drove as though chased along the near-deserted street. It seemed to be closing in on six o'clock, the tail end of a long summer day. The pain I'd kept by me, to keep me alert, threatened now to overwhelm me. "It was the only thing I could think of."

"Bees? Your life on the edge of a pit and you can only think of honeybees?"

"In summer, bees live about a month. They wear themselves ragged collecting nectar and pollen. Drones and queens live longer, except the drones who mate with the queen and the ones left in the fall. They die."

"So will you, and you will take me with you."

"You will drive when I go back in a couple of days."

I saw his eyes flick to the rearview mirror and cloud back to the road. "The bees will be better passengers than you!"

"Take me to the Paris. Is it open again?"

"Of course. But the prices have gone up."

"Take me."

61.

Andrea was at the same table we sat at before. She had only one glass in front of her. Everyone else in the bar eyed me worriedly as I wobbled between the tables. My bandage marked me as a target, one some enemy had already come frighteningly close to hitting. I could see them thinking they'd rather be behind the marksman than the mark.

But Andrea smiled in recognition when she caught sight of me. Her smile washed away when she got a good view of my color. "You look terrible."

"It's good to see you, too."

"You ignored the doctor's advice. You should have rested."

"I rested last night. His pills make me woozy. I need to be alert."

"It's not smart, Ron. What happens if you can't function?"

"Whatever would have happened if I never came?" I cracked out a pain pill and swallowed it with a swig of Andrea's gin-and-tonic. "Harbison lied to me."

"I knew he would."

"Just the porn, nothing more, he said."

"You didn't argue with him?"

"Only when he said he thought I should go to Israel for treatment, join the people who dropped me off. I told him no."

"And what did he say to that?"

"Something cheery, like 'It's your funeral.' "

"So what's next? What did you find out?"

"Nothing more. Nothing I'm going to tell you."

"You can, you know."

"It won't get me anything. It won't get you anything."

"Don't be sure."

"I know you know things you can't tell me." Her head flinched to the side, like a sympathetic reaction to a blow to someone else. "I might need the same privilege. How intact is your diplomatic pouch?"

"You saw what it was like at the airport."

"I don't mean coming in, I mean going out."

"The safer it is, the more the hassle. For a lot of hassle, I can keep it safe."

"From our own people too?"

"That's just luck. They have the right to look at what our government claims protection for. Only makes sense; you don't want some sour foreign service officer dragging drugs into the country on diplomatic immunity."

"Yeah, I guess."

"Why do you want to know?"

"I want you to carry something for me."

"Where? When?"

"Whenever you come to the States."

"A couple of months. We rotate. What have you got? A pound of hash? If you say yes I'll be very disappointed."

The pill, or the alcohol, or the exhaustion with the pain itself numbed me. I receded within, puppeteer to my burned and scarred shell. It scared me; I'd always been so much my body. I craved a drink to quell the fear, but feared the alcohol would shrink me more. "You'll have to trust me on it."

"Trust you? It's my job on the line, Ron."

"It's not illegal to carry if you declare it, I can tell you that."

"But you don't want me to declare it. That makes it illegal, secret."

"You keep secrets. That's what makes you trustworthy."

"A secret like what was on the tape."

"OK, so you're not trustworthy. I trust you anyway. You earned it."

"So how will you earn my trust?"

"With results. If I free Elizabeth, will you trust me?"

She wavered, but acceded. "What do you want me to do?"

"Just come to my place the day after tomorrow, just like you did yesterday morning. Keep the package I give you safe until you can take it to the States."

"To be safe I'll have to carry it myself, you know. It'll be months—July, anyway."

"If you can keep it safe, I don't care if it's next year."

"And if you don't get results?"

"It won't make much difference to me then, will it?"

"That's crazy talk. I mean if I doubt you, not if you fail."

"Then the package is yours. Do what you want with it."

62.

I slept like death through a night that never cooled. Flies began to buzz around me before dawn. I remember thinking or dreaming: This will be the morning I will not wake up. But nothing is as relentless as the mechanics of a new day. The sky bloomed grey-blue and searing. The early heat of the day allowed only for slow motion. I rose like a blister, watery and painful.

First I called Brian. Gone for the day on family business, back tomorrow.

I went to the American compound to check in with Harbison, who made me wait in the heat before he'd talk to me. "Still here, Stutzer?"

"Yes, sir."

"Hoping to get shot at again?"

"No, sir. Just checking in, like you said to. But I do plan

to leave the day after tomorrow. I thought you might want
to know."

He thought he'd won. He's a military man down to his
bunions and like Elizabeth said, they always need an enemy. He couldn't help but show the pleasure of his victory.
"It's for the best. I said it before, you're an amateur playing
in the big leagues. Not a bad showing, for a plug. It's a
rougher game than your Saturday softball group, isn't it?"

63.

The telephone office baked like an oven. There were no
cool spots. The walls were even hotter than the air.

I called Jacobs again. "I think I'm almost ready to clear
out."

"Ron? Is that you?"

"Yeah, I'm almost ready to clear out. A few more days."

"Are you sure? We can come and get you now, you
know."

"No, I've come all this way, I might as well stay a little
longer."

"You're giving up?"

"They want more than I have to give them. At first I
thought I could handle it, but it's much more and much
worse than I imagined."

"Well, I understand. No one will be disappointed. You
gave it a shot."

I looked around the booth. I swear I was followed, but
that's all right. They have people at the bank, people at the
phones, people everywhere, almost. I caught the eyes of a

few people I thought might be tracking me and smiled at them, a smile like a wink. Who knows if they understood, or even cared, or even knew who I was. But I would rather die knowing I did my best than wondering if I missed a detail somewhere. Of course, I'd rather not die at all.

I asked, "Anything I need to do at the bank here?"

"I don't think so. No problem with the money?"

Thank you, Noah Jacobs. "Yeah, perfect. I'm going to the bank now. I expect I'll have all five."

"When do you want us to come?"

"I'll let you know. Just wanted you to be ready is all."

"Ready any time you are."

64.

I have never before offered someone a bribe, never before knew of anything worth bribing someone for, never had the resources to build a big enough golden slide to give someone else's morals a ride. And my own morals, coming down to it, never would let me induce someone else to shrug off theirs.

I spent twenty minutes with my grey banker, who looked cool in his Western suit. I had papers to sign and accounts to check over. Throughout, the $200,000 sat beside him on the desk, a simple brick of bills; but enough to buy a house, some land, some quiet—at least in a country where none of them seemed portents of blood. On my letter of credit, he worked out the accounting. I'd converted close to half of my half-million dollar limit. He handed me the letter of credit and the brick. I began to count.

When I got to $190,000, I stopped. My banker's face formed a question. "I need an accounting error."

"Excuse me, sir?"

"Today is Friday. You will be closed over the weekend. Can you grant me an accounting error until Monday morning?"

"Sir, we cannot plan an error."

"But sometimes errors do occur?"

"Why, yes."

I separated the remaining bills from the stack, $10,000 worth, and set them on the desk between us. "May I borrow your pen?"

"Of course."

At the end of the figure at the top, the initial figure, the $500,000, I added a 0. "I need nothing—just an extra zero in the accounts between now and Monday morning."

"I cannot do that."

"How much remains in my line of credit?"

"Over two-hundred-fifty thousand dollars sir. You can see, it's there."

"And how much for the error and your silence?"

He clouded over. "Until Monday, not beyond?"

"And I'll ask for the balance of my credit now." He squinted at me, ready to object. "I will thank you now for your help. I don't expect to see you again. You may do what you like with the balance."

"May the error occur at the end of the day today?"

"You will need to make it as you fill out your papers on this transaction." I wrapped up my $190,000. "I sign this receipt for $200,000, and you give me a zero."

I signed my papers and laid my banker's pen on the $10,000 stack of hundreds. He took both and said, "Allow me a few moments to prepare the demand note for the balance of your credit."

"The balance?"

He paused. "The balance of the first half a million dollars in the line of credit."

Everything was simple after that. My banker did not even examine my signature on the demand, which relieved me. I signed it with Harbison's name.

65.

Friday afternoon I went to the hospital again. When you realize how bad even special treatment can be in places like Lebanon, you forgive the humiliation of illness in the States. Sure they have X-rays in Beirut, but I swear my head got bombarded by the exact same machine that my leg did when I pulled some ligaments in a high school game in Cleveland more than fifteen years ago. And the Lebanese don't just snap your picture, give you a bad magazine and then tell you what's wrong. I had been X-rayed two days before, and they just got the results back Friday morning.

The doctor with the thin slick hair pulled himself away from his ward of youngsters mangled by random violence when someone's bomb—or maybe even their own—exploded close enough to take a digit or a limb. He had tsked over me when he had changed the bandage and personally supervised my photo session. I was the doctor's prize patient. Maybe I'm one of the few who survived.

"And how do you feel today, Ron Stutzer?"

"Hot," I told him. He looked alarmed.

"Let us hope your trauma has not led to infection! I must prescribe you antibiotics!"

"No. The weather."

He laughed. "Oh yes. Hot!" Then he put on his mask of concern. They teach that in medical school. "But relating to your injury, how do you feel?"

"Either numb or in pain. If it hurts, I take a painkiller and the pain goes away."

"You must be careful of those pills, Ron Stutzer. They are codeine, very addictive."

"Thanks for telling me."

"You are most welcome. I have reviewed the X-rays we took yesterday." He had a light board behind him, a small one. It was illuminated, but it was also blank. He made no move to bring out his pictures for me to see. "You recovered from some significant damage to your knee many years ago, and now there is only a bruise there. Also there is good news about your jaw, which must still hurt but encountered no broken bone. Very lucky!"

"And the ear."

"Your left ear had less luck. I could tell when I saw you Tuesday at night that you would suffer disfigurement, slight scarring on the neck and punctures to the cartilage on the ear. Also the burn on your neck—does it hurt now?"

"Like a blister."

"So, some scarring there as well. For your hearing, I do not see complete recovery. The damage is small. The concussion of the shot dislocated one of the hearing bones, and I would recommend surgery. But even so . . ."

"Surgery?" This thought truly pained me.

"Not here, of course, goodness gracious no. But when you return to the United States of America, there you should have surgery, though I cannot say what sort of recovery your hearing might receive. But you hear perfectly on your right side?"

"Yes." Acrid sweet gas, knives in my head: I felt woozy from the image.

"And you have had no dizziness?"

Except for now? "No, no dizziness." Was he going to recommend going under for that too?

"Then the damage is simple, though perhaps not reparable. Of course, the sooner you see a specialist, the better for you. Until you can leave the country, I say rest, rest, rest."

66.

I could take the doctor's advice overnight at least, though my rest was delayed by a message Hussein gave me as I arrived home. Mr. Brian Bowman had been looking for me.

I called him. "Can you give me all day tomorrow?"

"Funny you should want me. I was at a conference for the family business today, and my job is to help you in any way I can. Our *pro bono* work. Noble, aren't we?"

It couldn't have been much later than seven the next morning when I arrived at Brian's house. I only had to wait for Andrea to pick up the packet I had wrapped up for her.

"You won't tell me?" she asked, bouncing the brick in he hand.

"Trust me," I told her. It was all I could say.

Brian was dressed down in jeans and a plain linen shirt, but I could tell that both of them had been recently pressed.

"I like the way it came out."

"My hair? Well, I'm stuck with it for a while either way. Not too Eurotrash?"

I didn't know what he meant. "No," I said. "It's perfect."

"I've got some coffee prepared. Are we going to work hard today?"

"Very."

"Then I'll order us some eggs and ham. One of the advantages of being part of the Christian establishment, our servants work Saturdays. And they serve ham without a whimper. Now, what's the plan?"

"I'm going to need a few things from you. To start with, six beehives."

"Not a problem, of course. Isn't that a lot of honey, though?"

"I don't want the honey. In fact, I'm going to harvest all the honey in the hives. And I'll need twelve queen cages."

"What's a queen cage?"

"It's a small wire cage, about the size of your fist, with a plug hole at the bottom. When you want to introduce a new queen to a hive, or if you want to stop the queen from laying for a while, you put her in the cage. That way, the bees can be near her, but they can't get to her."

"No more hanky-panky, eh?"

"No. Queens mate only once. But bees are touchy. If you disturb the hive, they might kill their own queen. The cage protects her."

"So twelve cages for the queens."

"No, six for the queens and attendants, another six for scavengers."

"What for?"

"I'd rather not tell you."

"Fine. I understand. You run it your way and I will help. What else do you need?"

"An open truck for the beehives and a driver who is not afraid, either of bees or guns."

"The truck we have, the driver we do not. All of the people who work for me fear guns, except Hussein's boys, whom I can't trust to drive. And I'm not fond of bees."

"So what do we do?"

"Can't your driver take the truck?"

"No. He has to take me in his cab."

"Well." Brian quietly snorted in and out. "Do you suppose you can protect me from the bees?"

"Sure, of course. But why?"

"Because I'm not afraid of guns."

"I'm sure you've got a keeper's suit somewhere. It covers you all over."

"The kind with the veil over your face?"

"Yup, that's it."

"That won't do. I'm not afraid of guns when the people who carry them can see my face. My face is my passport in Beirut."

"We can protect your face with alcohol or something. Bug spray, cold cream. You won't be exposed to bees and guns together very long."

"You have a plan, don't you? This is not an experiment in beekeeping?"

After breakfast we went to the apiary. Hundreds of hives, bees everywhere. The head keeper followed us each step, explaining what I already knew, but in Arabic. I told Brian again what I wanted and he translated for me, into both French and Arabic, to make sure his man got it right.

I wanted the keeper's most aggressive hives, the ones that collected the most honey, flew the farthest afield, defended their hive and queen the best. He disputed each choice, reluctant to give up his best producers. I could see the lies in his eyes; beekeepers have no skill at deceit. We were suited up, but the man in charge insisted he handle the hives. I watched him as he first smoked the bees into submission. Something about bees and smoke—they fall into a trance, a stupor. Smoked bees hobble deep into the hive and sleep.

When the buzzing dipped to a hum, the keeper pried the frames from the super and shook the dozing bees out of combs and into the hive. A few of the more energetic ones jerked their way to us and tried to find a place to attack. Brian tried batting them away, but they gave up on their own and went back to the smoky hive.

"Tell him to put empty frames back in the middle." I wanted the hive to lose their brood; nothing excites a hive more. The beekeeper argued with Brian that it would destroy the hive, at least that's what his gestures seemed to mean. So I walked in and started handling the frames myself. All the frames with brood I held between my gloved hands and pushed against the comb with my thumbs until the comb shattered. The keeper saw that I wasn't afraid, that I knew what I was doing. He relaxed his objections, directing the boy with the smoker here and there, just as I needed. After a while he smiled. He had no teeth.

We returned the harvested frames to the edges of the hives and put the ones I had broken in the center. We hunted down the queen and put her and a dozen of the youngest looking bees with her in a cage. The queen cage fits in neatly at the top of the hive, where the queens like to stay most of the time anyway. Then we closed off the entry. The gathering bees, the ones who came back later laden with nectar and pollen and who arrived at the landing board expecting a welcoming committee, got a peculiar reception: human hands sweeping them into another cage. They disgorged their harvest as soon as they realized they were trapped, gathered together and waited where we put them, near the queen as possible, but outside the hive.

It took most of the morning to prepare six hives and load them on the old red Ford with wooden slat sides. I felt sorry for the beekeeper as he watched us drive away with his Control Towers, his prizes, his babies.

67.

After a failed attempt at a midday nap, we met again at Brian's house, Brian, me and Amir too.

"This man is crazy," Amir said to Brian when he surveyed the truckload of bees. "I am truly sorry he is a friend of yours."

"All great leaders are crazy. That's why we follow them. So, Premier Ron, what's the plan?"

We drove to Dahya in a tiny caravan, Amir in the front seat of his cab and me in the back, Brian staying twenty yards behind in the rattletrap pickup brimming with agitated bees. I had a honey-crate from the apiary on the seat beside me with the six queen-and-attendant cages in it. All the ride over I watched the attendants groom the queen, picking invisible dust out of the hairs on her back. Bees are fascinating, brilliant. There are dozens of species of bees of varying levels of social sophistication, from the ones who lay an egg and food in a hole in the ground and fly away, never to see their young, to ones like these Italian bees, organizing sixty thousand of their mates into a single goal. You never see a hive divide against itself.

Saturday, outside of East Beirut, is like Sunday in America's black ghettos. You ever walk around a poor neighborhood on a Sunday? Maybe it's because the ministers' sermons still echo in people's heads, or that the ones who never hear the sermons stay in bed late after a wild Saturday night, I don't know. But those places where even the buildings seem to threaten you feel full of odd goodwill on a Sunday afternoon, somehow cleaner, friendlier, more open.

Most of Beirut was like that Saturday afternoon. It took a manageable amount of imagination to see it as a paradise.

The boys at the checkpoints were lazy-lidded, uninterested in my passport, kindly even to my bees. They looked, don't get me wrong; and they had their guns. But they didn't shove the muzzles all the way into the car, just rested them on the sill of the open windows; they didn't pretend they might confiscate my passport, just compared my photo and my face. They didn't haul the bees out of the car, break down the crate, smash the cages. They just looked in and smiled and joked. One checkpoint waved us through without a glance; another stood unmanned. The buildings which had appeared on my earlier drives to be inert rubble showed sign of life. Men gathered in doorways and children buzzed in and out of invisible crevices.

As we pulled up to the checkpoint in Dahya, I looked out the back window. Brian found the turnoff behind the gas station and timed it perfectly. I don't even think the gatekeepers noticed his truck. They just watched Amir coast to a stop beside their guns. I glanced at my watch: ten minutes to four. Perfect.

Even the Dahya guards lost their edge on the Sabbath. They expected us, of course, checked our passports and papers, even asked us out of the cab so they could pat us down. Amir showed them his gun, under his hat on the front seat, and they laughed and teased Amir. He translated, "They think this gun will not shoot. They may be right. It never has."

Then they wanted a look at the bees. For people who eat so much honey, they seemed ignorant and fascinated. You would think a dozen bees in a small cage would be commonplace to them. I was afraid they would shrug their shoulders, rattle the cages, agitate them, but they didn't. These were boys, like boys anywhere, absorbed easily by the mechanics of something so small. I couldn't have intrigued them more with a miniature tank or a pile of gold.

It took nothing but Amir's help in translation to make them a gift of one of the cages.

I caught sight of the first of the hunter bees as we got back into the old Mercedes. I needed heroics from them. They were my best hope.

"I wish you would explain to me just how I am going to lose my life," Amir said. "First you make me drive to Dahya with a car full of bees, and then you give the bees to the people who will kill us."

"You don't need to worry about it."

"I was worrying for my father, who would hate to lose his son."

"You remember what we planned?"

He drove along the same main street we'd driven along before. He slowed near the place we'd parked the car before. "Of course. I park by that arch," he said, pointing across the way, near where I'd seen the boy disappear before. "I leave the car running, but go under the hood as though it needs repair."

"And if the guards come?"

"Of course they will come. They will come and beat me senseless with their guns."

"Amir!" The nervousness, the pain, made me jumpy.

"All right, all right. I ask them to help. They won't; it's Saturday. You will come back in forty-five minutes minutes, we drive away."

"I will come back, go away ten more minutes, maybe more. If I'm not back in twenty minutes, you leave."

"Without you?"

I didn't answer. I didn't want to think he might, or that he might have to. Amir stopped the car and looked back at me. I ignored his gaze and stepped out into the dusty street. I cradled the crate against my chest, warmed by the hum of the workers in service to their queens.

68.

The moment I entered the square I was surrounded by Avai's guard. His gun-toters were men always, not boys. They had survived the petty skirmishes at the checkpoints, raids and kidnappings. Crazy eyes look the same in any land, and these men had them.

They wanted my crate. An American walking through Dahya with a crate will excite anxiety, Sabbath or no. The oldest of the lot said something I took to mean they would carry the crate for me. We walked in a cadre to Sheik Abdul's, the man with the crate beside me, men with guns in front and behind. If they had wanted to kidnap me they could not have contained me better. I was their man, but I seemed the only one who knew it. They were an honor guard, and I had the momentary thought that the people who stopped to watch our procession would break into a cheer. Of course they didn't. They were as silent, as unsure, as I was.

Avai was at the same table we had occupied two days before, but the cafe was empty except for him. He stood as I approached and welcomed me by indicating a seat. He had no interest in shaking my hand.

"Good Sabbath, Mr. Stutzer. It is a good day for peace."

"Yes, Mr. Avai."

"Sit, sit. I must have a look at your honeybees."

I sat. Avai peered into the box in his guard's hands and examined each cage carefully with a thick prodding finger. His nails were barely stubs, ragged and discolored. The bees satisfied him and he waved his guard across the narrow alley. The group retreated to the far wall and took turns studying the cages.

"As you said, honeybees. I have told your friend that there was perhaps some progress toward her release. She seems quite knowledgeable of honeybees."

"Yes. I told you they were a hobby of hers."

"True, but the words of a man with something to gain must always be suspect. Surely you have learned this, even in a land as free from strife as America."

"America is not so peaceful as you might imagine."

"We do not imagine America is peaceful, Mr. Stutzer. Too many of our compatriots have died for our believing. But still, life in America compares with favor to life in a land fought over."

Across the way, guards broke into laughter. One was holding his finger and jumping around, as if he'd been poking his finger into a cage and a bee stung him. Which they might have.

"Mr. Avai, I am told that bees suffer in extreme heat. Could they be delivered to my friend now? I'm sure she'll take it wrong if the bees arrive weak and sick."

"Yes, certainly. These men are clowns." He waved over a guard and explained what he wanted done. I hope he told his guard to bring the bees to Elizabeth, but I had no way of knowing what he told him—destroy the bees, hold them aside so there is no trick, set them free. How could I know? And what choice did I have, but to go on as I had planned, hoping Avai took his honor seriously? Two guards walked off to the square with the crate and the remainder splayed out in protective formation around Abdul's.

"You will have a coffee and specialty?"

"Yeah, thanks."

Avai gestured to Abdul but said nothing. His gesture meant enough. I wondered then, thinking back to the café on the corniche, why a man of such importance would tail me himself, contact me, meet me outside Dahya. What

sort of power did he have, or confidence in the people below him, or faith in the importance of my presence?

The coffee and cake arrived at once. "I asked Abdul to
prepare this today specially, despite the Sabbath. Koran
teaches that you may work on the Sabbath only if your
labor serves the higher goal of peace."

"I'm not much of a man for religion."

Avai's eyes showed compassionate condolence. "So
much a loss for you. Faith gives a man strength."

"Does it have to be faith in God?"

"God maintains the faith you give him. When you give
your faith to yourself, or your beliefs, or another, you
must give and give and give. It is like throwing water in a
well."

"You speak like a clergyman."

He bowed his head. "It is an honor to receive a compliment from an honest man."

Honest? I said only, "Thank you."

"We see you have convinced your people to forward the
money you need."

"It is very difficult to bargain with you when you know
how much I have to spend."

"It will prevent our wasting needless time on small matters. We have set a price on your friend's freedom, and you
will pay it."

"I have already spent much of the money available to
me. Will you accept a quarter of a million dollars less than
five?"

"Only because I have accepted your goodwill, Mr.
Stutzer. It is what you have. You cannot pay more."

I put my hands on the table and glanced down. I didn't
want Avai to know I was looking at my watch. Four-thir-
teen. I needed time. "How will we make the exchange?"

"As long as you trust me, it will be simple. But you have
gotten ahead of yourself. You do not yet have the required
money."

"I made the request. I'm told I can't be sure I'll get it before Wednesday."

Avai sighed. "We do not like to keep women captive, Mr. Stutzer. It offends us. This is why we have been so willing to negotiate with you. We know your friend is a woman of enormous wealth and great intelligence and beauty. In most Arab households, it would be an honor if she accepted hospitality. But to keep her a prisoner? This we do not do easily. If it must be so many more days, so it will be. You are quite right, you cannot be certain of receiving the money before that day."

"So what shall we do?"

"We will keep it simple. At ten Wednesday night, you will drive to the same checkpoint in Dahya. We will stop you twenty meters from the checkpoint, where an unarmed man will see to the money; please bring it in a simple sack. We will assure the road will be quiet while the money is examined. That done, I will walk with your friend and you will walk with the money. We will make our exchange and go our own ways."

"May I bring a guard?"

"Do you fear you will need one?" Avai looked hurt. "With so many weapons around, it will be difficult to keep the exchange so simple."

"Can I have some time to think about it now?"

"Of course. Yours is a cautious response. Bravery requires caution. This is how we know no fool can be brave."

I didn't care for bravery, I cared for time. I rubbed my brow with the heels of my hands and flicked an occasional eye to my watch. Avai sat, eyes closed, a hint of a hum settling in under his breath. Minutes crawled. My sweat bubbled from every pore with the slow patience of dew forming on morning grass. I wished I had a pot to boil water; the time would have gone faster. Four twenty-seven. I watched a bee buzz at my plate, but I couldn't know if she belonged to one of the queens I'd brought for Elizabeth. I hoped not: I didn't want the hive distracted by honey.

I couldn't hold out longer. My left ear throbbed. I could feel it growing deformed underneath the bandage.

"Yes," I said. "All right, Mr. Avai. Wednesday night at ten. No guard, a simple exchange."

"Good, very good. We will not have a chance to speak again, I imagine. It is never easy managing these matters, but doing it so with you has given great satisfaction."

"Thank you." I wished I understood what he meant. I felt like a missionary in a boiling pot, swimming around in a hunt for the coolest corner.

"Will you have another cup of coffee before you go?"

I could have kissed Avai then.

"Absolutely."

When I left Sheik Abdul's, my watch said four forty-one. Avai's guard did not follow me out into the square, and neither did Avai. He stayed behind, humming verses of scripture to himself. I swear I heard a hive buzzing over his throaty mumble.

69.

I strolled unwitnessed through Dahya. It's true I didn't walk far, but in that short measure I seemed to be taken as a prophet by the people. An aura of peace spread around me. I saw no guns, soldiers, no hostile faces or scared eyes. The big square washed with people and I was a bubble on their waves, carried intact above it, unnoticed.

I turned left off the square, down the main street which

led to the checkpoint. The hood of Amir's cab was up and the engine coughed and hummed, but the only company he had was a squadron of small children, whom he mock-threatened every now and again. They scampered back from him when he did it, and then courageously ventured an index finger close enough to the cab to provoke him again.

I looked at my digital. All fours. Just right. I stared up at the sky above the cab and caught sight of one, three, half a dozen, half a dozen dozen bees! It was too hot for them to fly, normally, but for the bees, the situation was anything but normal. The queen had been kidnapped!

Brian seemed to have followed his simple instructions: Park in the lot behind the gas station. He should immediately open the six queen cages holding the gatherer-bees from each hive. They'll look for their queen, being carried through Dahya's streets to Elizabeth. In about twenty minutes, the first of them should return, dancing with news of discovery. By then, the hives should be opened. Wearing his protective suit, out of sight, Brian should bang the hives until all the bees join the hunt. More of the first group of hunters will return with more information. More bees will fly. When they've all gone, then Brian can just get in the truck and drive back home.

"Having car trouble, Amir?"

"Nothing you didn't tell me about before. Have you spent your five million dollars? Can we go home now?"

I squinted down to the checkpoint. One of the guards was looking our way, but I couldn't tell what he saw. Another guard began swatting around him. "It won't be long," I told him. "I'm going to sit in the back seat, for half a second."

And I did, in the street side door and out again the other side. The raised hood and the open door covered me as I dipped into the alley under the arch. I looked up. A phalanx of bees spiraled overhead and then dove deeper away from the main street. The alley I was on ended in another, narrower one. I jogged left and then quick right. Another wind of bees, a larger one this time, headed off to my right. Ten yards down the new alley I turned off right into another. I kept my eyes up, trying not to lose track of the bees.

The unconcern people had shown me in the central square faded now. A clatch of old women sat in the first doorway, knitting and telling lies. The click of the needles stopped when I rounded their corner, and they fell silent. I ignored their stares as I struggled through the narrow alley. Above, the bees disappeared in drying laundry. When the little walkway ended, I was stuck at the cross of the T, following my own weak discretion. I heard shouting to the right, a pair of ten-year-old boys shouting and pointing. A voice from behind them called out from the darkness of a house, scolding them to silence. I scampered to the left, away from them. There, above, a line of brown bees aimed like a dart straight ahead, maybe a bit right. I flew like they did, eyes up, down a one-house alley. I stumbled out into another square, a small one, a little fountain, two shops, two cafés, old men everywhere.

The fathers and grandfathers looked up from their back-gammon games amazed, stunned. A shout started some-where in the square, and then laughter. An old man nearby, beard white and scraggled, smiled up at me from his low stool. His tunic was a dirty grey and his one front tooth horse-yellow and turned sideways. He kept his hand close to his chest, but still he pointed to the next alley over off the square. I winked at him. He nodded, smiled again, and folded his hand away like a precious, oft-read letter.

I ran, now, flat out, but no one followed me. Out into the square just enough to reach the next alley. Who knows what damage I did on the way, tables upended, premature heart attacks? The men in the café I skirted watched me only briefly. They kept their eyes pinned behind me. They saw I had no gun. Could they be sure my pursuers had none? But no pursuers arrived, and no gunfire, and no catastrophe except a slight disturbance in a long Saturday afternoon. I must have disappointed them.

The next alley was long and nearly straight. It chasmed like a canal for forty yards off the square. The buildings crammed side-by-side shops, but they were all closed, doors blocked tight. There were no locks, anywhere, and very few young men. All at the mosque? All dead? All working for Avai, guarding Elizabeth?

I choked. My God, what have I done? I'm deep in the hive of my enemy, lost, unguided. I am even wary, I realize, of my goal, my Elizabeth. Will she recognize me? Will she come with me, leave the safety of capture for the risk of escape? The buildings in rows around me grew tall and narrow, three storeys and just five yards of the alley between them.

Ahead, the alley breaks slightly to the right and then goes straight as far as I can see. At the break there's a walk to the left. As I near the walk's corner, I see them, I hear them. The swarms, the competing, buzzing, stinging swarms.

70.

The walkway is dim, even in bright sun, but I see the place right away. The second house in on the right, two storeys high, no guard out front. No problem knowing why, either. I hear the frantic shouts in the upstairs window. The bees are rampaging in a brown cloud in and out the upper windows. The first wave has found their queen, surrounded by bees from other hives and swinging startled humans. Just sit still Elizabeth! Just sit! There's panic in that room upstairs. The guard from the door must have run up to settle it and fell into the panic himself. One hundred thousand bees! More! Panic, of course!

Another brown cloud appears over the roof of the house across the street and tears in the open windows. The shouts get higher, the panic more pronounced. Someone's head appears at the window, shouting. His arms flail; he has no gun.

Two teenagers, one dragging his gun by his strap, explode in a tumble from the door and tear off past me, right beside me, a knife blade away, but fear has replaced their sight. Both brown faces are blotched with welts, and a few dozen more bees are in pursuit. One bee takes a moment to sting me. I could have crushed her, as I watched her land on my hand, prevented the sting, but the smell of her blood would arouse her hive-mates. I accept the venom; the pain is nothing compared to the burn of a bullet.

I hug the right hand wall and move quickly along. I'm hunting the ball-carrier, it feels like. The field's gotten smaller, but the search is just the same. I freeze outside the doorway. Inside I hear a scream and a leap. One's coming downstairs. I tense, hunker down. Deep breath. Tighten! Tighten! Spring!

I laid my right shoulder into his kidney. I felt the air going out of him, like a blow-up soldier. Fast as a cat, I lifted myself off of him. He was maybe eighteen, same kid who'd flailed at the window, no gun. He didn't breathe the moment I looked at him, but that's was only the wind I'd taken out of him.

I clambered up the stairs, saying nothing. I wanted to shout for Elizabeth, hear her voice, embrace. But I had no idea how many people remained to guard her, how many guns. The bees fluttered thicker than autumn leaves. I held my breath and squinted my eyes against them. I needed to move slowly or be stung entirely.

In the first room a man balled up on the floor screamed. His gun rocked on the floor behind him, but he had his face to the wall and his hands shielding his head. He kept kicking, like a mad dog set on him instead of a thousand bees. Three hundred stings will kill a man and I thought that one might die. He thought nothing of me, didn't seem to know I was there.

In the next room there was a bed, a table, a chair. The small square room was in the middle of the house, dark, no windows. It smelled of old food and sweat, shit and piss, like an old school gym they use as a cafeteria at lunchtime. On the bed a lump under an old thin blanket quivered. I kept feeling the little pricks of stings, one, another, another, very slow. I was fine, if I could get Elizabeth now and go.

"Elizabeth!" I whispered. The lump rolled. I hissed again, "Elizabeth!"

She sat up. I never thought I would say it, but she looked horrible, like a pale brown mouse terrified into fatalism. Her green eyes looked old, like oak leaves just after they drop. I would have opened my mouth to shout, but the bees would have taken it for a new hive and buzzed right in.

But she doesn't know. She shouts, "Ron!" a hoarse, hoary croak, like she hadn't spoken for a week and wasn't sure she had the strength now. Then her finger goes into her mouth to pull out the invader. She shudders. She was a sorry mass of terror, a fluttering child having nightmares about the familiar.

In an instant, I gather her up in the blanket she used to protect herself from the bees. There were probably dozens wrapped up with her. She was light, tense, squirming. I carried her through the room with the dying man, whose protests had shrunk to moans and half-hearted kicks.

At the top of the stairs I set her down. "How many guards?" I hissed. She didn't hear me, she didn't see me. I shook her, I might have slapped her, I can't remember. "How many guards!?"

"Four."

Then we got them all, I thought. Three out the front, one communing with the bees. "Can you handle the stairs?" She nods. I start down ahead of her, skipping almost, but keeping slow and steady. At the door, the bees begin to dissipate, fighting each other, saving their queens.

The light outside makes me squint. I look back at Elizabeth. The light blinds her.

I step out into the alley.

One of the two who ran blindly by me, the one who held onto his gun, now holds his gun on me, barrel to my chest.

I grab the muzzle with my right hand, push it up.

He pulls his trigger.

Elizabeth screams. My index finger burns as I tear the gun from his hands. I whirl, lash the butt of the weapon into the side of his head.

First I feel the crush of bone up the muzzle.

Then I feel the burn.

I drop the gun and it lands on top of him. He was in almost the exact position I had left the other one before I'd gone up, but that first one was gone now, burrowed into some hole somewhere, moaning, and the second one wasn't going anywhere. Blood came from his ear and nose. His eyes didn't close, but they didn't look anywhere either.

I grabbed Elizabeth by the wrist and ran off to the right, away from that little square, away from where the guards had gone. The walk ended at another long straight alley, wider that the other one, also walled with closed shops. Overhead, I saw a trail of bees, the young ones, the slow fliers. Dead ahead I saw the beige open dirt of the main street, of escape. I dragged Elizabeth through the alleys, back to Amir's cab.

71.

Elizabeth was huddled and shrunken. She kept herself swaddled in her blanket, though the heat of Dahya roasted us. I led her like a dog, barking out "This way!" and "Hurry!" as though that was all she could understand—and it might have been. I felt certain we would run into Avai and his men at each corner that cut into our alley. I knew they would think nothing of gunning us to the pavement. The one gun already fired must have alarmed the prayer-peaceful neighbors. Could pursuers be far behind?

We lurched against the bees. We headed where they came from. At least they knew where they were going. If you mix together different species of bees in the same hive, they'll accommodate each other, but they'll never learn to speak the same language, they'll always misunderstand the other's gestures. Like the cities people build: I understand DC, but I'm lost even in familiar parts of Beirut.

The bees took us where they'd come from. I followed them backward. Only after we lurched out into the main street did I realize they weren't coming from the cab, but from the truck, fifty yards from Amir to the checkpoint and then another hundred beyond.

We burst onto the open dirt road like thieves, out into the bright and unprotected sunlight halfway between the cab and the guns. The guards were occupied with the bees who were after the queen in the cage I gave them. Of the four there before, only two remained. Their faces, rubbled with bees stings, seemed from my distance to hover on the edge between wonder and terror. They squinted at us through the cloud of bees.

But they didn't see us blunder into the street, not the guards anyway; I couldn't say about anyone else on the street. The twenty-five yards between us and cab looked like forever. Amir, leaning his head into the engine hood, looked under his left arm and saw me and my shrouded ghost approaching. He almost called out, but stopped himself. He scattered the few remaining children with a threat, but one kid slammed shut my open door when he left.

I knew, watching the door swing shut, that the click it would make would sound to the checkpoint like the cocking of a gun.

I began to run again, dragging Elizabeth, a rough sack, as devoid of will as the blanket she hid under.

Amir knew too what the slammed door would do. He slammed shut the hood and whipped himself into the driver side. "No!" I shouted "No!" I didn't know what he was doing—escaping without me? whizzing the ten yards to get us? The movement would confirm what the door-slam made the checkpoint suspect.

But there was no room for observation down by the checkpoint. The remaining guards were too stunned by the bees to add up the scene fast. Amir's tires spit dirt stopping beside us. I hurled open the back seat and shoved Elizabeth in. "Down on the floor!" I jumped in after her and tried to look composed, sitting like just another fare in any cab's back seat. But there were no other cabs in Dahya, and there was no price on the meter for dangerous escapes. "Drive slowly, Amir. Drive like we're just going home."

Amir tried, I'm sure he did, but with his head turned

back to look and one hand under his hat feeling for his gun's trigger, the car jerked ahead. My door slammed shut again with our forward thrust. I looked back and saw Avai's guard pursuing now, at last and too late. They saw they couldn't catch us on foot and opened fire from behind.

I dropped like a pail of water all over Elizabeth; the bullets would get me, not her. Amir slunk down in the seat and gunned the engine. "Those machine guns, they shoot a lot but not well."

The checkpoint! I knew it was coming, but I couldn't see when. I tried to figure our speed, the distance, anything! We'll get there NOW! NOW!! NOW!!! At that third NOW we must have, because the inside of the cab exploded simultaneously with a shower of glass and deafening crack. Having been so close to a gun-muzzle, I knew Amir had blasted someone through the windshield. Then the cab hit some high gear and we disappeared from Dahya, its piety, its shouts and its gunshots.

72.

"I killed one of them, I know it!" Amir gloated. "At the checkpoint! And they scoffed at my gun!"

I pulled myself up to the seat. The burn in my hands jangled me. I flopped back into the seat exhaustedly, my arms vibrating like chimes. The entire left side of the windshield had flown everywhere with the bullet's impact, and the right side hung veined and limp as a fresh road-kill.

I tried to help Elizabeth to the seat, but she wouldn't

budge on her own, and my arms had no strength. I had helped her all I could.

I held up my hands to inspect the burns I felt across my palms. The burns were there, but the tip of my index finger wasn't. I gasped for breath; I think that's the only thing that kept Abdul's coffee and specialty down.

I couldn't keep my mind from reviving the experience. Hand on the muzzle, the shot, the burn in my finger—that was it, I must have held the tip of my finger over the black hole! Then wrenching the gun free and swinging it like a bat through the ball of that man-boy's head and then the burn on my hands, and the god on the ground, the crush of his skull now burned into my hands with the hit. A home run, we're on our home run now.

I ripped the cuff off my shirt and wrapped it around what was left of my finger. I said, "What about the other checkpoints?"

"What?"

I realized I had hardly hoarsed out a word. "The other checkpoints."

"Do not worry about the other checkpoints. We had no trouble coming down. You really got her, you really did!"

I looked down to the floor, holding the remains of my right index finger in my left hand. Yes. I got her. Amir was right. Amir skirted backroads and neighborhoods up into the Christian hills to avoid the Lebanese Armed Forces at the green-line. The checkpoints we hit gave no trouble: only two were manned, and Amir slowed down for them, but then he floored it before the casual gods could get their thunderbolts warmed up.

"To the embassy?" Amir asked.

"No," I told him, "Brian's. Take us to Mr. Bowman's."

73.

Elizabeth began coming around as we drove up the last hill to Brian's house. He must have alerted Commander Faid's men that we might be coming back with a prize, because they picked us up safely past the last checkpoint. I'd never had an armed escort before. I never felt worse in my life. But Elizabeth perking up warmed me, brought some feeling back. Given how I felt, this was like any answered prayer: better not asked for to begin with.

"How are you doing?"

Elizabeth settled herself on the seat next to me. "Better, I guess. A little."

Amir said, "Better than in the hands of those pirates! Much better!"

"This is Amir, my driver."

"You're hurt." She noticed first my hand, then my ear. "What happened?"

"He's a hero, that's what happened!"

"I'll tell you later," I told her. "Now rest." She did, against me.

Brian met the car in front of the house, the first time I had ever seen him act like a regular person, coming out to greet company. But even that he couldn't let pass without a dash of gallantry. He opened Elizabeth's door with a flourish and helped her out. "Amir," he said inspecting the windshield, "you seem to be having car trouble."

That's when Elizabeth threw off the blanket and looked up at him. "Brian Bowman?" she asked.

"Of course. I've called for a bath for you." But Elizabeth was already around the car to me, as I negotiated between the pain in my hands and the door handle.

"Do you know who he is? Do you know?"

"Someone who helped you out. Does anything else matter?" She didn't say any more, but tore away from me and went toward the door, into the waiting arms of Brian's butler.

"What was that about?"

Brian shrugged. "Family business. You have to tell me all about your escape."

I examined Brian's face. He had not one bee sting. "All went well from your end?"

"Not a problem worth reporting. I had to dump the hives out of the truck when the sluggish ones wouldn't come out. I rolled the windows closed before the launch so the cab would be clear. Hot, but clear. Hopped in the truck and took off. The checkpoint guards seemed preoccupied when I left." I nodded. "I'll have a bath drawn for you too, and some food. Which do you want first?"

74.

The stings and her bath made Elizabeth drugged and sleepy, so I helped put her to bed. "Not a good man," she mumbled to me.

"Who?"

"Bowman. Family trades hashish everywhere. Them and the Gamayels, the Hamadis, they grow and sell. They run the Christian Phalange for profit. They're bad people."

"You wouldn't be free without him."

"Watch out." Elizabeth curled deep into the bed. "He owns people. The General . . ."

What about the General? She was slipping into dark sleep. "Elizabeth? What about the General?"

"The Syrians. The Syrian Army has him east, in Beka'a." She drifted off. "Not done yet . . . ." She was gone, unwakeable, captive again.

I sat on the bed with her ten minutes, holding her hand gingerly with the uninjured tips of the fingers on my left hand. My right hand curled in my lap like a cold cat. Brian's people had dressed the wound as best they could, and Brian himself had sent out a party from Faid's contingent to rustle up my doctor. I had gulped two pain pills and two snifters of brandy. The world was becoming a narrower place, it seemed, and one thing remained to be done.

"Where is Amir?" I asked Brian. He sat out on the terrace where we talked that first time I came to his house. I floated. My eyes held to their narrow focus.

"Tending to his car. We have to decide how you want to handle this release. It will only be minutes before word gets to the embassy and Harbison and then to the press. We need a strategy."

"I need to find the General first," I said. I got the whirlies as I walk back in the door, through the house and out front toward the car. I knew Brian had followed me, because I could hear a echo of his voice in thin protest.

"Amir," I called. "We have to get the General in Beka'a." I saw him look past me, back to where Brian's voice murmured to me.

"Go where?"

He came toward me. "Beka'a. Elizabeth says he's in Beka'a."

Amir pulled his gun from the back of his waistband. "We cannot go to Beka'a."

"You can't go. I can go." I brushed past him to the driver's door. I saw the glint of the gun behind my head and heard Amir say something to me, but I could not tell you what. I didn't hear. I was too busy falling to the ground from the jolt of a gun butt smacking my head.

75.

It ought have felt like *déjà vu:* the same room, the doctor, Andrea, a guard by the door. But this time the guard had his gun at the ready, Andrea sat sulkily in a corner, and the doctor was talking to Harbison and Amir. The room hummed with artificial light; the shades on the windows were drawn, but I could tell that nothing but deep black night lay behind them.

And at least this time I could talk without trouble. "Where is Elizabeth?"

The doctor, Harbison and Amir froze with their eyes cast suddenly to the bed. Andrea sprung out of the chair to my side.

"She's debriefing in the Embassy. She came here on a State Department detail, so they claimed first dibs on her."

"Is she all right?"

"All right?"

"She's not hurt?"

"Oh no, she's fine. Except for the stress of a week as a hostage, and the pain and poison of the bee stings."

Harbison advanced to the foot of the bed. "That will be all, Captain."

Andrea stood and tossed a half-hearted salute. She was wearing her uniform and looked very military, but she gave her Colonel no answer.

Amir came to the other side of the bed. I tried to sit up

to face him, but the lightening down the back of my skull made me flop back. "I'm sorry I hit you," he said. "You're so much bigger than me I really didn't have a choice."

Harbison said, "That's enough, Captain." I flicked my eyes to Andrea, but she was just settling back down in her chair. Amir acknowledged the command with a mumble. I shot him a question with my eyes, but all he could muster was a shrug.

"So you see, we didn't leave you entirely on your own," Harbison said, "though Amir tells me you would have gotten your friend out even if he hadn't been with you."

I looked at Andrea, who rolled her eyes. She looked bleached, as though she'd received a bad scare not long before. I wondered how I looked.

Harbison said, "The doctor is very discouraged with you. You should have been taking it easy." I saw the doctor's slicked-down head bob. "But we're very pleased with you, very impressed."

"Thanks."

"We owe you the thanks, not the other way around."

"A whack on the head is your way of saying thanks?"

"What's a little pistol-whipping between friends?" I could tell by the way he lifted his invisible eyebrows that Harbison thought this was a stone riot.

"So what do you want me to do for you?"

"You've already done enough, son, we don't need you to do anything more."

I wished I could stand up to face Harbison. "You don't have the guard at the door waving his gun around to protect me, do you?"

"Actually, we do. Word of your actions travels fast. There are a whole lot of people out on the street who wouldn't mind killing you."

"This is new?" I'd felt like a target since I'd arrived in Lebanon, like it was always night, I had a spotlight on me, and strangers shot at me from the dark.

"Three car bombs since dark, that's my count." Harbison turned to Amir.

"I think four. I just heard a rumble a little while back."

"Amir has good ears for car bombs; he's set a couple in his time. And a van of insurgents unloaded some ammunition at our gate patrol just after dark. Some people here are very unhappy with you."

"But not you."

"Me? What do I have to complain about? You freed the girl and you're both safe. I would have preferred no one got hurt, of course, but . . ." He opened his hands in front of him, as though he was helpless, a supplicant. "But there is one small thing you can do for us, as I think about it."

I laughed, his ploy was so obvious.

"When you tell your story, will you leave out that Amir works for us? This really isn't so funny. He won't live long if they know he's an American soldier."

"How long will he live anyway? If they're after me they're after him, too."

"I suppose that's so."

"So why do you want to stay out of this?"

Harbison put on a face of forced confession. He leaned forward on his arms and supported himself against the bed frame. "You got me there. You sure are right. The truth is, we feel our operation here is secret and we'd like to keep it that way. It's important that it continues to appear that the US has no military presence in Lebanon."

"Important to you."

"Important to all of us. Important to the free world."

"And Amir?"

"We'll reassign Amir somewhere safe. We just want to make sure no one thinks the liberation was our plan. It wasn't. You know I tried to stop you, and I'd hate for it to appear to the American public that we were trying to take credit away from a man as brave as yourself."

He wanted me to believe this so badly that I agreed—no

mention of Amir's connection, no involvement of the Army or Marines or whatever branch Harbison belonged to. Of course, I didn't believe that was all he wanted. I just believed he would keep on talking at me until I agreed, and I couldn't stand it.

76.

The doctor examined me, the Colonel debriefed me, Amir apologized to me, and no one left me alone for a second. They would not let me see or talk to Elizabeth, who they claimed was either busy with her work or sleeping. I couldn't sleep for wondering where and how she was. The doctor eventually gave me a shot, he claimed for the pain, but if I had to bet, I'd blame Harbison's desire to keep me quiet. I can't say I minded the shot that much, though. Having the tip of your finger shot off hurts more than you might even imagine, hurts like sand in your eye, but there's no way to stop the pain, except with drugs.

The doctor harrumphed about my hands and my head and said he was certain that the wallop Amir gave me would ruin any chance I might have had of recovering my hearing. I was hardly listening, only waiting for the salve on my palms and the drugs to ease my pains. "You will have to spend a week in the hospital in Tel Aviv," he told me. "Do not expect to go home for at least a week."

And Harbison said, "I gave your people a jingle, and they'll be here in the morning to take you home."

But the mention of home just made me long for Elizabeth more, and the Colonel's questions about street names in Dahya and the position and layout of the house where

Avai had held Elizabeth only irritated me more. When Harbison took the doctor aside, and Amir made his tenth attempt to apologize, I knew I was in for a sedative. Maybe I was asking for one all along.

They never left me alone with Andrea, but as I was sinking into the medicinal haze, she sat beside me and held my left hand. "You really proved something," she told me. "You really did."

77.

Oddly enough, the battalion that escorted us to the airport Sunday morning encountered no resistance. Even I offered none, though Harbison and some other official-looking people insisted that Elizabeth and I ride in separate cars. Safety, they said, protection. Maybe the drugs the doctor shot me with still coursed through me, but I felt grey as a cold wet day, though the weather was anything but. Summer had arrived in Lebanon with fearful vengeance. I couldn't imagine the sun would do anything to cool the fire between the warring sides.

Jacobs was not on the plane, but I can't say that surprised me. Instead, we were escorted by a contingent of American guards and a military psychologist. At first I figured they must have thought I was crazy for doing what I did, but the brain doctor was there more for Elizabeth than for me. The head of the guard drippingly told me that we could use the conference room after the plane cleared the range of ground-launched anti-aircraft. No one fired on us, no one wanted us that badly.

Except the psychologist. He introduced himself. "I'm a

specialist in post-traumatic stress disorder, PTSD we call it. People in high-stress or in war-like situations, such as being held hostage, experience a checklist of resultant after-effects, such as deep identification with the oppressors."

I tuned him out. The guy wore a uniform, Air Force I think, and talked like someone trying to sell Congress a new weapons system. He talked for the full forty-five minutes the flight gave him.

Elizabeth said, "Like a transference of parental relationships?"

The shrink said, "Exactly," and droned on like the engines. Elizabeth seemed to pay close attention. Maybe something he said made some sense to her. Maybe she saw him as a puzzle and tried to figure out what the duck was yammering about. Who knows, maybe what he had to say came close to her experience.

Or maybe she just didn't want to talk to me. I sure got that feeling. Most of the time she just acted like I wasn't there, accepting a hug when I offered it to her, but accepting it the way you accept a bellhop's help with your coat.

When the plane set down we taxied near the terminal, but we didn't get out. Jacobs came on instead. He replaced the psychologist, but what he said was just as nearly incomprehensible. "The press is waiting inside. I've briefed them—"

"The press?" I asked. "What the hell for?"

"To cover Betsy's rescue. It's news, Ron. You're news."

"I don't want to be news."

"I'll handle them," Elizabeth said. "I'm more used to it."

"They want something from Ron."

"Will a photo do?"

"The photo goes without saying, but they want some words, some kind of statement."

"I'll make some excuse, his injury, the stress, something."

"Can't he give a statement, just a couple of sentences?"

Elizabeth at last looked at me, but she didn't ask me a thing. "I'm sure he can." Her eyes were flat. For the first time in our life together, I noticed the thin trace of a wrinkle around her mouth. Smile lines, but she wasn't smiling.

"Can you handle that, Ron?" Noah asked me, as if I had just suddenly appeared. "A short statement, that's all. How happy you are to have done your job well, looking forward to recovery. Nothing much. Can you do that for us?"

"And a picture?"

"Yeah, you can't stop that. They'll be snapping bulbs at you even before you enter the room."

"Hell." I looked at Elizabeth, who was ducking her head down to glimpse out the porthole windows. "Sure, I'll make a short statement. I don't want to answer questions."

"Fine. No Q&A."

"Can you keep the whole thing down to five minutes? We haven't been left alone since I blacked out."

"I'll try for five, but expect closer to ten."

I shook my head in refusal, but I knew I had no power. I was the hero, sure. That only meant I had to play my role well. No rewrites.

"Your father will be here in an hour."

"My father?" I gulped. But I saw Jacobs was talking to Elizabeth; he pointed his chin at her in answer to my question. A rush of embarrassment trampled up my back, rekindling the burn on my neck.

Elizabeth smiled now. "Good. I can't wait to see him."

The press conference matched my imagination. Cameras flashed from all over, and we had to stand on a podium so everyone could see us. The picture you all probably saw was Elizabeth and me caught in the crush at the door, my hand raised, Elizabeth seeming to lean back against me. I think she was bowled back into me by the flood of the room's excitement.

Noah introduced us with a lot of fluff and I said my little piece, but Elizabeth was the star. "You'll have to forgive Ron. He's not only injured," she told them right off, "he's also the strong and silent type." People laughed and clapped. After the tension of the week, the sound came over me like peace. Elizabeth portrayed herself at the podium as the woman I lived with, the woman I'd gone halfway around the world to free. She charmed the press and told them nothing at all about what really happened.

On the way out I said something to her about it, and she whispered to me, "Why give away for free what you can sell later?" I turned to look back at the podium. My back creeped as though we'd left our own ghosts up there behind the microphones.

78.

We all went right to the hospital, a vast and modern place, as clean as the one in Beirut was dirty. Everywhere we went, the American guards went with us, and the psychologist. An Israeli detail guarded our guard. Elizabeth and I were separated again for our exams, but we waited together while they ran the tests to see if I was fit for surgery. I wanted to talk about her, how she held up, how they treated her, but when I asked she said, "Me? Look what they did to you!"

"They didn't do this to me. I did."

"You didn't have a gun. You couldn't have shot yourself."

Then her father came in, straight from the airport. He

didn't look like he'd spent twelve hours travelling. Did he have two planes like the one I'd travelled on, another like the one that fetched us?

The door frame seemed to expand around his bulk. He wasn't even as tall as I was, I realized, and small-boned under his weight. For the first time I noticed his face had a skew to it, as if the left side always attempted a poor imitation of the lead right. He didn't grumble now, he almost bellowed, "My little girl!"

Elizabeth bolted up and threw her arms around him. We were both in johnnies and hospital robes and I imagined the feel of her near nakedness pressed so close. "Daddy! You're here!"

"And you're safe?" Elizabeth nodded but couldn't speak. Her arm around his neck reached up to cover her own face. I stood up slowly, embarrassed wearing so little in front of the Grumbler. I could see clearly now: Elizabeth was crying, at last. She might have cried while we were separated, I don't know, but she hadn't cried to me.

Jacobs came in the room and brought a chair up for Elizabeth's father. Elizabeth would not let go of him as he comforted her with whispers, "My Betsy, my Betsy." But still he found a way to free his right hand and extend it to me for a shake. I held up my bandage and gave him my left instead. He nodded his head toward his daughter and said, "I didn't think you could do it."

Most of me wanted to say, Then why did you send me? I said, "I wasn't sure I could either."

"I will never forget you for this, son. Never."

"Thank you, sir."

"Roger. Call me Roger, Ron. Let's all sit down."

Roger led Elizabeth to her chair, between us. Though she sat, she wouldn't let go of his guiding hand.

"This is her first cry," I told him.

"Well, it's good for her." With his free hand he petted her

hair, which seemed to bloom back to its rich color under his touch. "I have some news that might cheer you up," he told her. "On my way over here I got word that the General returned."

"Her General?"

"Watkins? Yes."

"I thought he was dead."

"Obviously not." Elizabeth sat back and let go of her father's hand, but still she said nothing.

"Well, who freed him?"

"Freed him? No one. From what I gather, he just drove away."

"Drove away?"

"He wasn't captured at all, it turns out. He was in negotiations with the Syrians all along, secret negotiations. The kidnapping, the ambush, that was a cover."

I looked at Elizabeth. If the General had been involved in negotiations, Elizabeth would have known he hadn't been killed, hadn't been captured. So why the hell did she go to Lebanon in the first place? "They staged it? They staged the killing, planted a story about the General being taken hostage?"

Roger shrugged. He pointed to Elizabeth. "This is the family expert on the Middle East. I suspect she knows the purpose of the sham."

"What about her?" I asked Roger. "What about you?" I asked her.

Now she spoke. "I can't tell you yet."

"I risk my life going after you and you can't tell me whether or not you were really a hostage?!"

"I was really a hostage. You really did get me out. But I can't tell you anything more until I hear what happened with the General."

"I don't understand," I said to her, and then to myself: "I just don't understand."

Nurses and orderlies flooded into the room with a gurney. Elizabeth said, "I just don't know what I'm allowed to tell you yet. I don't know what's protected."

"From me?" I felt myself almost shouting. "Something's protected from me?"

"Now settle down there, Ron."

I burned. "I feel like I earned a little respect here!"

"At the expense of national security?" the Grumbler shot. "Respect gives you the right to shout at my daughter?"

I raised my hands in concession. The head nurse called my name. I nodded to her and got up. "We can work on this later. I want to know. I deserve to know."

"You'll know what the government thinks is safe for you to know," Roger mumbled.

"Dad," Elizabeth cautioned.

"He shouldn't yell at you."

"Ron's got surgery now. Go easy."

Her father looked chastised and stood up. "I'm sorry. We're all under a lot of stress. I haven't slept for two weeks." I thought I saw Noah smile from his position by the door. He put out his hand again. "Good luck."

I shook left hand to right, like before. Elizabeth joined us, putting an arm over each of our shoulders. She kissed her father's cheek and then mine. "Good luck," she told me. "I'll be here after you get out of surgery."

I felt my knees begin to quaver, muscles pushed past endurance. I had wanted to walk down to surgery, but neither the aides nor my legs would let me. They helped me on to the gurney and rolled me away. It was late Sunday afternoon when I left Elizabeth and her father standing side by side, surrounded by aides and guards and nurses. The sun was just rising Monday before I was conscious again.

79.

I don't know if you've ever had surgery, but I'm amazed that so many people have. You feel like Lazarus as you come out of the ether or whatever they feed you to keep you temporarily unaware of the damage the surgeons inflict. When I eased into wakefulness everything was black-and-white, like my dreams; I couldn't will myself to move, like sleep. But in dreams you don't have peripheral vision, and in sleep the impotent muscles aren't in your bladder. The liquids the doctors fed me in the operating room now wanted out, but my head couldn't find the switch to make it happen. I began to cry, tears streaming hot and sweet, not salty. A nurse came in then—it was a single room and I think she was assigned to very few patients—and said something to me I could not hear.

"I wanna pee," I rasped. She took a dull red pitcher from the table beside me, the only thing with color I could see, and slid it under the covers. Her hand laid me gently over the rim, and we just waited for something to happen. It wouldn't. I cried more, could not speak. She said something more to me I couldn't hear but somehow understood: Did I want a shot for pain? I nodded, I think. She rolled me over like a balloon and pricked me. I disappeared until full day.

80.

I woke because of my bladder. The nurse was there before I could do anything. She motored the bed up and arranged the pitcher. Whether it was the angle or my returned control I don't know, but it felt like the liquid inside me contained whatever drugged me, and as it streamed out I became more alert. Color returned to the room. I could see it was just me and the nurse.

"Elizabeth?"

"Your friend?" The nurse had a stiff accent I took for Israeli. "She left word she had meetings all morning at the Embassy. She asked me to call when you were awake."

"She said she'd be here." Tears came again, I couldn't stop them.

"She will be soon, I promise."

I took a pain pill with breakfast, and then the doctor who operated came in. It was the first time I had met him, except for a brief hello as the staff prepped me for his knife.

He was short and square-faced, with rectangular glasses that sharpened the corners of his head. He looked barely ten years older than me and spoke with a Midwest twang I recognized as Western Ohio.

"So how are you feeling this morning?"

"Worse than I did when I came in here."

"Temporary, I can assure you. In a couple of weeks you'll be feeling much better. Any pain in the ear?"

"It's hard to tell."

"The pills will make you groggy, but keep taking them until the pain stops. That'll be about a week."

"What does it look like in there?"

"Small and red." He smiled, and his glasses rode up on his cheeks. "You had some permanent damage to the inner ear. All we can do now is wait and see how much good the surgery will do you."

"Will I get my hearing back?"

"Not all of it, but if I'm as good as people tell me, you'll get back fifty percent, maybe more. A hearing aid can give you the rest. It looks to me you won't hear sounds in the lower registers no matter what, how low I can't say. That's the part of your ear that took the most damage. Gunshot?"

"Right next to my ear. Dirt kicked up from the bullet."

"Must have been keeping your ear pretty close to the ground. You might want to see this."

He laid a *International Herald-Tribune* on the bed table. The front page had that shot of me and Elizabeth captioned, "Lovers reunited after a daring escape." The headline read "HEROIC RESCUE IN BEIRUT," and then under that in small type, "Millionaire's Daughter Unharmed."

At the bottom of the column, a story in a box was headlined, "AMERICAN GENERAL ALSO RELEASED," and then, "Details of Capture Uncertain."

"I never repaired a hero's wounds before," the doctor said. "I feel honored."

I stared at the stark white bandage in the photo, the tired smile, the injured eyes. "What about my face?" I asked. "What about my ear?"

"I didn't do much in the way of plastic surgery. I was more concerned with the function of your ear than its looks."

"How bad does it look, really?"

"Even with surgery there'll be scars. Not on your face so much as your ear. It's always going to look a little bit like a dog's chew-toy. Cartilage just doesn't heal the way soft tissue does." I raised my right hand. "Neither do fingers. We cleaned up the wound for you, sewed it over so it will end up smooth, but the tip was gone and there was really nothing we could do."

I began to fade out again. I felt like a cripple, or like my father, hanging onto his bottle-crutch even though it only protected him from himself.

"Just think of your scars as medals for heroism. No one can take them away from you, no matter what. You earned them, and you'll keep them."

"Yeah," I drawled, nodding out. "But what will they cost me?"

81.

Elizabeth did show up, sitting there when I came to that afternoon. She looked wonderful, hair bouncing with independent life, eyes flashing concern. She was reading a file of some kind, as near as I could see. I didn't mind interrupting her. "Hi, Elizabeth."

She held up a finger to me. Patience; she must be in the middle of a paragraph. She folded the file and put it on the seat next to her.

"How are you feeling?" She came and perched on the bed. I wanted to hold her hand, but mine was too sore. "I'm sorry I couldn't be here earlier, but I needed to debrief with the General."

"Is he here?"

"Came in last night."

"Is he all right?"

"Tired, but fine. Like me."

"Can you tell me what happened?"

"A little bit. Are you up for it?"

"As much as you can expect."

"OK. But stop me if you get tired or don't understand, OK?" I nodded, but was certain I wouldn't understand and couldn't be made to. "The General went into negotiations with Syria, I can't tell you what for. They were supposed to be secret. Secrecy was Syria's request; they didn't want to risk their ties to the Soviet Union."

"Russia? How did Russia get in on it?"

"They didn't. They're not. I'm just explaining the secrecy. Having the General 'kidnapped' covered his disappearance."

"OK. What about our capturing the hash?"

"What about it?"

"Was that real?"

"Certainly. It showed what we could do, if we had a mind to. Brings out the interest in negotiations."

"So why did you have to go to Lebanon?"

"Because, though the press didn't know what was going on, the leaders of the other interests in Lebanon did. At least, they knew that there were negotiations, not what they were for. So they began to threaten all-out war, in private meetings, unless we cut them in. I went to help in the negotiations with these other groups, but one of the militias decided that having a hostage put them in a better position than being told second-hand what other people were negotiating for. I got to be the hostage."

"They gave you away?"

"Who?"

"Us. The Army. Harbison."

"The Colonel? What does he have to do with anything?"

"Anyone, then. Were you set up? Why you?"

"No. We knew they might take someone. But then, that's always a possibility in Beirut."

"What about Brian?"

"Brian Bowman? He's nothing. His family controls a huge amount of trade in Lebanon, plate glass, weapons, tires, anything that moves fast in a war zone. We weren't in Lebanon for the money, I can tell you that. We had nothing to do with the Bowmans."

"So I really did free you?"

"Absolutely." She kissed me now, and I thought I might fly off again. "I haven't thanked you yet."

"I'd do it again."

"You will not." She said it with more vehemence than play.

"Well, don't get taken hostage again."

"I don't think I'll get the chance."

"Did something happen? Something go wrong?"

"The big deal didn't happen."

"With the General?"

"Uh-huh. Once the Syrians got the news that I was free, they shut down talks. I think they saw that Lebanon has too many factions, the place is too unstable to control. Of course, the publicity scared them off. News meant no more secret negotiations. Syria needed secrecy, and we couldn't give them that any more."

"Is this going to cause you problems?"

"Me? Personally? No. Lebanon? Probably. Who can say?"

"I hope it causes them big problems. It's a stinking place. I hope I never hear about it again."

"I don't think we'll be so lucky."

"When do we go home?"

"Not tomorrow. Maybe the next day, maybe the day after. We're just waiting for you to stabilize. The doctor said it should be all right to fly, as long as we keep the cabin pressure up. Daddy's other plane can make the trip in one shot. He took the one you flew over on back already."

"So it will be just us?"

"Yes, just us. And the General."

82.

Except that I was recovering in an Israeli hospital, the next few days went on like days at home. Elizabeth worked, and we visited for a couple of hours each day. I wanted to see her more, of course, but I always wanted to see her more. I slept and made my slow climb out of the chasm of anaesthesia. By the time I was fit enough to fly, I no longer felt like I had died and returned. My ear and finger still hurt like hell, and the pain medication doped me more stupid than usual, but at least I didn't feel numb. I don't think I'll ever look at death as an attractive respite again, not if it feels anything like that.

Though I felt like I could walk easily enough, medical attendants wheeled me out of the hospital and from the car to the plane. The surrounding soldiers kept reporters at bay, I noticed. On the plane I asked Elizabeth, "What about the reporters?"

"We've been keeping them away from you. So you could recover."

"They must be printing something. They sure haven't forgotten about it."

"We gave them an official version; they still want to talk to you. I want you to meet the General."

He came on board with a coterie of uniformed eagles, men my age or so, but with eyes that seemed to constantly scour the landscape for food. Parabolas constructed the General's face: a swoop of chin and jowl, a permanent frown for his lips, a sad droop to his eyes. He came right to me, and I struggled to stand. I thought he might expect a salute.

"Take it easy, son," he said to me. "Nobody has the right to expect anything more of you for a time to come."

Elizabeth said, "General, I'd like you to meet Ron Stutzer. Ron, General Watkins."

"An honor," I said. I meant it; I had never met a general before. What surprised me most was that he had big, flat eyes. I expected narrow, glinting ones.

"The honor's mine, son." He sat beside me. "In my business, we deal with heroes as a matter of course, but most of the heroism I've seen comes from people who simply don't run away when any common-sense fool would kick dust. To actually go out into danger, that's bravery. Not common sense, of course, but, dammit Ron, it's bravery."

"Thank you, sir." He didn't offer his first name.

"But I suppose any young man worth his salt would pursue a prize like Elizabeth." He beamed at her like a horse trader at a prize colt. "She's tremendous, I couldn't do what I do without her."

"It's easier to be brave when you know what you're after."

"I hope we're not just talking hormones here," the General said. "A strapper like yourself doesn't have to go to Lebanon for that."

Elizabeth jumped in. "Ron treats me like a queen."

"A queen bee, eh?" he laughed. "I'm going to order all my men to study them now. Can we train bees, maybe get them to help us out again?"

"I don't think so. You can only make it easier or harder for them to do what they're going to do anyway."

"Kind of like terrorism, isn't it?" he replied. "Every now and again you can wrench them, like you did, but mostly you can only make it harder or easier for them." He looked at Elizabeth. "Probably going to be easy for them for a time to come, eh, Elizabeth?"

"That's not Ron's fault, General."

"No, of course not, of course not. Well, I'm going to go check in with my pilot and then sack out."

He got up and walked to the back of the plane. I said, "The cockpit's up there, sir."

He winked at me. "Maybe, but the bathroom's not."

I could feel the grind of the jets warming up. I swallowed a pill I hoped would make me sleep the rest of the trip.

83.

The Washington airport shuddered with reporters. Even the police and Army folk couldn't keep them entirely at bay. How would the reporters respond if the boys in uniform actually unstrapped their guns and showed off that black hole at the end? I imagine they would have found another story more interesting.

I asked the soldier pushing my chair to stop just before we got out of the terminal. I saw a limousine waiting curbside. It was black, and I didn't want to get in it before I had a chance to say something. I stood, a lot easier from the high seat of the wheelchair than from the low ones on Elizabeth's father's plane.

Flashes and screams rose and then settled. Microphones appeared in front of my face from ten feet away, from nowhere. Elizabeth closed in to my side and I looked down into her worried eyes. That was another picture of us that ran in papers: concerned looks for her injured hero.

"What really happened in Beirut?" I heard a reporter shout. The others must have too, because the whole lot of them quieted down.

I said, "I got lucky."

Questions exploded again, but this time I quieted them

with my hands. "Beirut is a horrible and difficult place. What we went through was horrible and difficult. We both need rest and quiet. Can you people back off for a couple of days? I promise to tell the whole thing when we're feeling better. Is that a deal?"

A wide-mouthed woman, holding a microphone with a TV station insignia boxed around it, screeched, "Isn't this some kind of cover-up?"

"The only covers I want right now are on my bed. Please leave me alone. You'll know when I'm willing to talk."

Elizabeth took my arm, and I walked with her out to the car. The General got into the car with us, and first thing he picked up the phone. Once we slipped off into traffic, Elizabeth leaned against me and said, "You handled that well."

"I'm a regular hero. Will it work?"

"Work?"

"Will it keep them away for a little while?"

She shrugged. "I'll get the word out that people who bother you won't be invited to the press conference later."

The General smashed down the phone and creased a frown deeper into his flesh. He said to Elizabeth, "The news isn't good."

"What?" They knew the topic without saying.

"Iran has offered a thousand men in support of LAF."

"Direct support?" The General nodded. "What about Beka'a?"

"Pitched battle."

"Can you tell me what's going on?" I asked Elizabeth. She begged permission. The General tossed his hands in acquiescence.

"The Lebanese nationalist movement has picked up steam. People like the ones who kidnapped me used to support Lebanon as a country only if they were in charge. Now they seem willing to support Lebanon first."

"Isn't that good? It sounds good, like they'll have a country again."

"No, it's not good," she told me. "They want an Islamic Lebanon, run like Iran. But they won't get it, and the fighting will just continue."

"Bloodier," said the General. "No one will be in charge. I think we're even going to have to pull our people out, just throw the whole country to the wolves."

"What about the Christians?" I was thinking about Brian. "Will they be all right?" But neither the General nor Elizabeth answered for a while.

"They'll be all right," Elizabeth then said, "if they don't mind dying."

84.

Elizabeth installed me in the apartment and then went with the General to the Pentagon to work out the latest crisis. I could tell from the silence and the restraint that somehow my releasing Elizabeth had screwed up some plan for Lebanon our government would have preferred. Thinking about this kind of scheming always made me tired; with me tired already, this exhausted me. The news turned Elizabeth hyper. She had more energy after the limo phone call than she'd had any time since I'd last seen her at home. And how long ago was that?

The phone machine tossed me right back into my life. We have a machine that flashes a red light the number of messages you received. I couldn't keep count with the flashes, I lost track somewhere in the twenties.

I got a piece of paper and sat with the playback.

First call, from the people at VISA: Suspicious use of my credit card. I tested my memory: what had I done with it? Given it to my father that day he showed up. Maybe he tried to buy a liquor store with it. I took the number.

Then a call from Jim. Any news of Lizzie? Meeting with her dad? Control Tower showed the first signs of beginning to swarm. A new girlfriend on view if I could come that weekend.

Another call from VISA. Same information.

A call from Professor Nusanti. Back at Columbia, wishing me luck. Call him when I return. Number.

Then the phone rang. I halted the machine and answered it. It was someone from some magazine somewhere. I said, "For calling me at home, you get on the list of people who will not be called to the press conference."

"We don't want a press conference. We want an exclusive. Ten thousand dollars!"

"I've got your name. I might get back to you."

So I set the machine back up to answer the phone with a new blank tape and put the other one into the stereo. Terrible sound, but I could make it out if I turned the volume up. So now I could screen the calls and listen at the same time.

Mr. Bienenkorb. "Ron? I'm just calling to let you know I know you're OK. I'm getting calls from all over the map telling me not to worry about you. So I'm worried." Then he grunted for a while, like he wanted to say something more. He didn't, though, and the tape clicked to a dial tone.

Then Jim again. "Where are you? Any news on Lizzie? It's first thing Friday morning, figured I'd catch you before you headed off to work. It's muggly and ugly out here on the farm. If it doesn't rain we'll get a swarm today. Are you OK? I'm worried about you, man, deeply worried. So call me."

After the tape.

The phone rang again then and it was another reporter.

The next message was from VISA again, this time someone higher up, a different number and name, but the same problem. Friday afternoon.

Then Jim again. "If you don't call me soon I'm going to come hunting for you. Where are you? I don't get any news from any place. Help me out here. Call me."

And then Jim again, right away. "I forgot to tell you. Control Tower's out of c-c-control. The first swarm left yesterday, Friday. Half the hive. Now another swarm's getting ready. The queens are just letting each other be. What should I do?"

Phone again: Jim for real. I kill the tape deck and grab the receiver. "Jim!"

"Man, you there? That's you live?"

"And lucky to be that way."

"I can't tell you what a relief it was to see you were safe. I'm coming over. I want to see the hero in the flesh."

"I'm tired, Jim."

"Of course you are. You want to sleep, it's OK with me. I never seen a hero sleep either. I'll be there in an hour, just stay up 'til then."

Then, on the tape, the calls from reporters started. One after the other, names and newspapers, TV and radio stations, magazines. I didn't even write them down. But then came one call that really surprised me. A literary agent, called himself Kent Boomer, claimed he already had offers of fifty thousand dollars in advance against book and movie sales of my story. He left a New York number. I wrote it down. You don't know, ever really know, what you'd do for money.

The reporters had kept calling. One after the other, several repeats. One radio guy called the machine while I was listening to his message from days before. The stereo ID'ed the guy while the voice on the phone machine in the bedroom said, "I know you're there, I saw you go in, just pick up the phone. Come on, just pick it up. A quick statement is all I want, just a quick one. I'm not going to hang up until you answer." I turned down the volume on the phone machine and let him stew on the line. I don't know how long he stayed on; I went back to listening to the messages.

Jim again. "My hero! Way to go, Ron! Welcome home, Lizzie! I always knew you were a hero, but what about Ron? Surprised the hell out of me. So, Ron, why didn't you ask me to c-c-come? I wouldn't have, you know, but I would have come up with really good excuses. I love you both. Call me."

And then scattered among the reporters' requests were calls of congratulations, some of them from strangers, one from my mother, one from Bienenkorb, a whole lot from people Elizabeth knew sideways, I guess. Names I hadn't heard but who I could tell knew her or her family. Even Nusanti called again.

But then, between two calls from the same reporter, was this message: "This is Detective O'Connor of the New York Police Department. I am looking for a Mr. Ronald Stutzer. I have information which may relate to your father, James Stutzer of Cleveland, Ohio. Please call at your earliest convenience. It is eight o'clock Wednesday morning." His voice had a slow deliberate pitch to it, so the message sounded older than half a day.

I copied down the number and went over to the phone. It had the dial tone back. I pushed the buttons while I heard the tape say, "This is your boss. I just want—" before it hissed and clicked to a halt. Sometimes even a ninety-minute tape isn't enough.

85.

"Detective O'Connor speaking."

"This is Ron Stutzer. You left a message on my tape."

"Oh, yeah, Mr. Stutzer." He shuffled some papers. It had taken me ten minutes to get through to him. If I hadn't been tired enough to drop I would have gotten impatient. "Are you the same Ron Stutzer what saved that girl?" he asked, still sifting papers. "Ah, here it is."

I didn't want to talk about Elizabeth. "You said you have news about my father."

"I might have news. Is he missing? Have you spoken with him recently?"

I wanted to say, We've all been missing, but I couldn't. "I saw him here in Washington I don't know how many weeks ago. Then he disappeared. I didn't know what happened to him."

"I think we may have found him for you."

"Is he all right?"

"No, Mr. Stutzer, I'm afraid he's not." My head spun. I had been standing, but now I carried the phone with me to the chair by the stereo. "Are you there, Ron?"

"Yeah, I'm here."

"We don't have a positive ID on him yet. We found him early this morning, just after sunup. Looks like alcohol poisoning, but we need someone who knows him to identify the body before we can do an autopsy. I'm sure this is an awful thing for you, but could you come up to New York and have a look for us?"

"How did you get my number?"

"Just plain good detective work," O'Connor told me. "He had it in his pocket."

86.

"Man, you don't look anything like what a hero should look like."

Jim got there ten minutes after I'd hung up with O'Connor. Of course I'd go to New York. "I think my father is dead," I said to Jim.

"What do you mean, you think?"

"I just talked to the police. In New York. They have a body they think is his. I'm going tomorrow to see."

"Are you well enough? You don't look it."

"You look wonderful, too."

"You know what I mean. Lebanon is no party." The phone rang twice, and I didn't move to it. Jim asked, "Want me to get it?"

I turned up the volume on the machine. "I'm screening calls." Another reporter. "The life of a hero."

"Hey, now. Don't scoff. You done good."

I smiled. A compliment meant more from Jim. "I couldn't have done it without you."

"Me? You didn't even ask me for help!"

"Yeah, but you got me into bees."

"Bees? So what, bees? What are you talking?"

"Bees, the secret of my success."

"You are *not* bopping up to New York tomorrow if you can't talk sense tonight. What's this about bees?"

"The bees I used to get Elizabeth out."

"You better rewind. This is the first thing I heard of bees and I've read every scrap of news I could find on this thing."

So I told him, and Jim couldn't stop himself from laughing. "I can't believe they left out that p-p-part. What for? National security?" he wheezed.

"I guess no one would believe it." I didn't feel giggly about Beirut, so I asked, "What happened to the Control Tower?"

"Oh, bad news," he told me, calming down. "You got the message about the queens?"

"Yeah. What does it mean?"

"I didn't know myself until they started to swarm for real. I called my experts. Seems that sometimes, no one knows why, the swarming instinct goes out of control."

"Out of control how?"

"Well, n-n-normal swarms, a princess comes back from her bump and grind and, instead of killing the old queen, she takes off with half the hive, right?"

"Sure. So what went wrong?"

"The rest of the hive didn't kill the remaining princesses, like they're supposed to. One by one they grew up, got stuck, and took off with half the hive."

"Shit."

"No shit."

"Just took off?"

"Yup. Four times, five. I lost count."

"What's left?"

"Not much. Under ten thousand, maybe under five. Some brood, but not enough nurse-bees to raise it. The old queen keeps laying, but she looks mighty lonely."

"We could find one of the swarms, kill the new queen and put them back."

"I don't know where they are. I don't think any of them set up house in one of the free hives. Not yet. This just happened over the p-p-past few days."

"Oh, man." I sat down hard. Pain came back.

"Not been the best couple of weeks, has it?"

"The stuff I've seen."

"Where's Lizzie?"

"Work."

"You're kidding."

"Some new stuff coming down with Lebanon. I better call her, let her know I'm going to New York."

"Is there anything I could do for you?"

"Find some way to keep the press off my back until I figure out what's what."

The phone rang again, and another reporter begged to talk to me. Jim picked up the phone before I could stop him. "Mr. Stutzer has asked me to tell you there will be a press conference tomorrow morning."

Through the machine, I heard the reporter ask when. I flashed Jim both hands, fingers up. I meant ten o'clock. Jim spotted my wound. "Nine-thirty," he said. "At the Pentagon. Ask for the room when you get there."

I heard the reporter ask, "Anything else?"

Jim said, "Yeah. Spread the word." He cradled the receiver home, but upside-down, so it stood from the phone like a pair of mouse ears. His turn to ask me, "Anything else?"

"Uh-huh. Stick around. I need a friend. I need you."

87.

Jim stayed over and handled the phone, night and morning, and joyfully greeted Elizabeth on her late-night return from the Pentagon. Come day, she was up before me and on the phone to her father, asking for use of an Upper East Side apartment the family had held for decades.

"He said there'd be no problem using the place. The doorman has the keys, and my father will stop by tonight around eight to make sure you're comfortable."

"He doesn't have to do that."

"I know," she said, easing the adhesive off my neck so she could change my dressing. "I told him that."

I gritted my teeth against the pull. Before we'd left the hospital for the flight, my nurse replaced the post-surgical cotton, which had been in my ear for days. It felt like taking a Q-tip out of your left ear, if you'd put it in your right. Everything around the ear was sensitive but the ear itself. I still couldn't hear anything out of that side. I sat on the flat-top of the down toilet seat, sweating with fear of pain. "I hope I can get my hearing back," I said, "at least a little."

"I hope I can stomach your wound," Elizabeth said. But as she lifted the bandage off she blanched. I thought for a moment she was going to faint. She surprised us both by staying up. Applying the new bandage, she hardly showed the same sensitivity she'd shown removing it.

"I can get plastic surgery for it, Elizabeth. Once inside the ear heals and I'm well enough, I can fix it."

"It's all pocked," she said, but not to me.

The phone rang again, and Jim answered it. Elizabeth left me sitting in the bathroom, sweat-slick and recovering from the ordeal.

Never become a hero. Being one is even worse than what you have to do to become one.

"You want to talk to your boss?" Jim called out to me from the living room.

Jim sat bare-chested and shrouded with bedclothes. He'd made coffee already and answered phone calls—playing secretary for us. He'd slept on the couch without folding it out, a big man made stiff by the small space.

I took the receiver from him. "Mr. Bienenkorb."

"Ron?"

"Yes, sir."

"I take it you're not coming in today."

"I can't. I have to tend to some family business in New York."

"The media guys tell me you have a press conference this morning, that's what I meant."

"The press calls you?"

"I think they think Housing Characteristics is a CIA cover or something. They can't figure out what we do, so they figure we're spooks."

"Don't tell them I'm going to New York. I want them all at the press conference."

"Lie for you."

I gulped. "Yeah, I guess that's what I'm asking."

"Can you do me a favor in return?"

"What?"

"Don't listen to the other job offers?"

"What do you mean?"

"I've been getting calls for days, not only reporters, but the White House, Congress, private industry. They all want you, and I don't think it's to give you a medal."

"I can't promise anything yet, except you'll be the first to know if I stop working for you. How many days can I take?"

"All you need. Just call me every now and again."

88.

I shaved my moustache last thing before I left the house. I thought it would be even more a dead giveaway than the bandage. Every morning paper had that picture of Elizabeth looking up concernedly at me. I had only luck to thank that no one recognized me until I stood on the platform ready to board the train. Real people are more polite than reporters; they keep clear. I slept on the train and no one but the conductor dared to wake me.

I took a cab from Penn Station to East 77th, washed up, and then took another cab down to the police station. The headquarters in Manhattan occupies a triangular brick building in a nondescript neighborhood near Chinatown. Except that the streets were paved and the buildings more recent, the feel of the place reminded me of Beirut, as though the teems of people who once lived here had drained away. The buildings were shells, shed and abandoned.

At the front desk, a burly black woman asked me to fill out a form, checked the information against nothing and issued me a visitor's pass. She seemed reluctant to give me directions, so I just wandered into the maze of police-central, hoping to find O'Connor. Fortunately, police are people who stay alive based on the faces they can remember, so it wasn't long before one of them recognized me and ushered me to Detective O'Connor.

"Got a hero for you here, Frank," my escort boasted.

"Ron Stutzer?" O'Connor stood. He had the bulk of a football player and the fleshiness of a beer drinker. He came from behind the desk fast for his size and took my right hand before I could wheel it away. He felt the bandage as he squeezed and lifted it up for inspection. "Oh, sorry."

"I'm going to have to get used to it."

"You lose a finger?"

"Half of one."

"Don't worry about it. In another couple of months you won't notice. The wife got nicked by a runaway electric knife ten years ago, lost the same finger. Says she only misses it dialing the phone."

"I guess."

"Yeah, well, let's get the bad stuff out of the way first."

O'Connor led me to the elevator and we took it down to the basement. "This is the part I hate the worst of the job. Bad enough when you lose somebody to a bad guy the courts let free on a technicality, what can you tell the family? Or having to handle suicides, terrible what a subway car can do to a person. But dealing with the families on stuff like this stinks, any way it's cut. Nobody's doing anybody any good. In here."

We went from the dim and incandescently lit corridor into the white fluorescent brilliance of the morgue. The attendants floated around like ghosts, pads on their feet, white pants, loose white jackets.

"The doctor here?" O'Connor asked. Someone pointed to a corner office. "Lady coroner," the detective confided and then walked me over to her door. "Afternoon, Doc. We got a viewing."

She was Indian, I guessed, but her color had me thinking a moment she was Lebanese. I felt a freeze in my legs, but it might have been from the cold of the place.

"The Stutzer connection," she said in unaccented English. "Sorry for this. After a triumph, you come home to a mess."

"It's not your fault."

"I might deal with death every day, Mr. Stutzer, but I'm not immune to its effects."

"Go easy on the man, Doc," O'Connor said. I waved off the protection.

She pushed a button to unlatch a cold-storage drawer. The sheet on the body had yellowed a little, or might have just looked that way next to pale blue-whiteness of my father's skin.

"Yes," I squeaked, "that's him."

O'Connor and I traced our steps back in silence, but when we got to his office he brought out two glasses and poured generous shots from a bottle of bourbon he kept in his squat brown refrigerator. "I always need a shot of this before I do one of these jobs." I nodded at the glass in thanks, but I didn't touch it. Maybe it's growing up the way I did, I don't know. I just learned to never drink if you have to make an excuse to yourself to do it.

"What do you need to know?"

"Name, age, date of birth, place of birth, residence, social security number, when you last saw him, when you last heard from him, any illnesses you knew he had, any reason to suspect malicious intent," O'Connor read from his form. I told him all he needed to know. When he got to where to ship the body, I gave the name of my mother's church in Cleveland. She lived with him longest. I figured it was her privilege to bury him as she saw fit. O'Connor poured himself another stiff one before we finished. I had a sip to wash down a pain pill. He didn't offer me a second dose when he saw I hadn't dented the first.

It was just past six as I got up to go. O'Connor shook my left hand and clapped me on the shoulder. "It's a bloody shame about your dad," he told me, "but it shows even a drinking man can raise a son like you. I'm proud to know you."

"One more question. Did he have my credit card on him?"

O'Connor shook his flabby head. "He'd been robbed. No ID, no wallet, certainly no credit card. Just an address book, mostly blank, and a scrap of paper with your name and number on it. Just luck he wrote his name in the book and wrote your last name on the paper, or we never would have found you. Sorry."

There was a cooling mist falling grey outside. I waited a long time in it for a taxi. My driver's name was Amir, I noticed on the registration hanging over the glove compartment. I didn't say anything to him except the Upper East Side address.

89.

Elizabeth's father woke me from a nap on the couch. He let himself in with his own key; I assume he asked the doorman not to announce him. He sat in a cushioned, wooden-armed chair at my feet before I could pull myself awake enough to even sit up.

"Hello, Ron."

"Roger," I croaked.

"I want you to know something right off. I owe you a tremendous debt, one I can never repay. Any time you want something, you only need to ask for it and it's yours."

"Thank you, sir. I appreciate that."

"Don't be so appreciative until you hear me out." He shifted his weight around the chair, which creaked in compliance. "I don't like owing people things, and I don't handle it easily. So any time you want anything—and I mean this whether you continue your involvement with my daughter or not—you get in touch with my lawyer. Here's his card." He put a white slip at the base of the lamp beside him.

"Well, I hope we'll be seeing each other anyway, sir."

"Perhaps." He clapped his hands to his knees and hauled himself up. "I was sorry to hear about your father. I'll leave you in peace."

I moved to rise. "Let me see you out at least. It's your place."

"It's my place; I know the way. Please don't bother." He walked away, and I heard the door open and close before I could make myself steady on my feet.

90.

I worried that Elizabeth's father would mind a long-distance call, so I had the operator put it on my card. "Ma?"

"Is that you, Ron?"

"Yes it is."

"Where are you? Are you in Lebanon?" She was shouting as if I was.

"No, Ma. I'm in New York."

"New York City?"

"Yes, New York City."

"What are you doing there?"

"That's the reason I'm calling."

"You went to New York to call me?"

"No, Ma. I went to New York because I had to identify Dad's body."

"Your father's body?"

I waited a beat to make sure the news had sunk in. Then I said quietly as I could, so I knew she'd have to strain to hear. "The police called me after they found him yesterday morning. He had my name and number in his pocket. He drank too much, and he died out on the street."

"Your father always drank too much."

"I know, Ma. Listen, I arranged to have the body go to your church. I didn't remember the name of the priest so I gave your name. I'm sure they'll be calling you about what to do."

"Do? I don't know what to do." I could tell she was crying now, soft tears. "He wasn't a bad man, Ron. He was a drinker, but not a bad man."

"I know, Ma. Ma listen, are you OK now?"

"How can I be OK?"

"I know. Call some friends. Call your priest. Have someone around."

"What about you? You have somebody? Is that pretty girl with you?"

"What pretty girl?"

"That one you saved. I know it doesn't sound right right now, but everyone here is very proud of you. I have gotten calls all day to say how proud. And now the day ends on this note."

"It's bad, Ma," I agreed. And yes, I'm alone, I thought. "I'll be out there as soon as I can. The day after tomorrow."

"I loved your father from the first day I saw him," she sobbed now. "And I'm going to love him until I die."

"Me too, Ma."

When I hung up the phone I felt like a cold steel ball had lodged in my gut. It made me shiver and sob. I blearily dialed home; Roger wouldn't mind a call to his daughter on his bill. But the phone rang and rang. Jim never put the answering machine back on, and the noise echoed around the empty apartment. I wanted to call Elizabeth at work, but I couldn't for my life remember her number there.

I took two pain pills that night, one for my head and the other for my heart.

91.

The next morning I made a series of calls. First, to Elizabeth, full of sympathy and hurry. "We've got a big meeting this morning," she told me. "We're going to have to evacuate Beirut, the fighting is getting horrible. It won't change anything, but still they fight."

"Why won't it change anything?"

"Because the people who own the hashish still own the

armies. Like the Bowmans. They'll stay in charge, whoever gets killed."

"Did I do something bad working with Brian?"

"If you could have gotten me out without him it would have been better, yes. It would be better if I were still a hostage, in some ways."

"You don't mean it."

"I don't know what I mean."

"How about the press?"

"The fake press conference caused a huge scene yesterday, but at least you got away. You see my father?"

I wanted to hold that off for later. "Yes, he dropped by for a second last night. I'm going to have to go to Cleveland tomorrow."

"Your father?"

"It was him, yeah."

"Ron, I'm so sorry."

"I should have known that's where he was heading. I could have done something."

"Didn't you already do enough?"

"I guess. I don't know. What's enough?"

"You can't save everyone, Ron."

"But my father."

"Just take care of yourself, Ron. Call me from Cleveland."

I was going to ask her whether she would come, but we don't involve ourselves in each other's families. Roger made it clear he knew the rule. I wished I could forget it. "I will. I tried you last night."

"Not at work."

"I forgot the work number."

"Well, write it down so you don't forget it again."

"I feel like I have a huge hole in my head and everything keeps falling into it."

"It will be better soon. I'm sure it will. Call me, whenever you want."

92.

I called VISA to report the card stolen. The supervisor asked right off if I was the Ron Stutzer in the newspaper and forgave all the expenses. They had already put a block on it last week, he told me, when the odd uses came up to the credit limit. I didn't tell them I had given the card to my father. If they hadn't shut the card down, he probably would have found a hotel to die in.

I called the literary agent who called me. We arranged lunch. I told him to bring whatever contracts he wanted. The number he left on the machine put me to an assistant, so I knew he must have had some stature. I didn't really care. An agent would put someone between me and the people who wanted my story; that's all I wanted. I told him that over lunch. He gave me the contracts, he paid, he took me back to his offices, which were huge, two or three floors of a nice building. He wanted me to take the agreement to my lawyer, but I wanted fast protection, so I signed. Everything.

I called Professor Nusanti, who told me to meet him at his Columbia office at three. He was in a rickety old building somewhere off the center of campus. His cubby reminded me of all the professors' places when I was in school, but it was bigger and better furnished. Still, the walls were covered to the molding with untamed bookshelves and each flat surface had a sloping pile of paper perched on it.

"So, how is the returned warrior?"

"Injured," I offered my left hand. He took it without comment.

"Sit down on the couch. Relax, you look like you could use it."

I was going to mention my father, but there was no point really. I wanted knowledge, not sympathy. "So, can you tell me what the hell happened in Lebanon while I was there?"

"Aside from you nearly getting yourself killed and starting a new explosion of the civil war?"

"I did do it, didn't I? No one's told me what I did."

"Tell me the story."

So I told him as much as I could, as briefly as I could. I didn't tell much about the bees—he was incredulous—but I described everything else the best I could.

"Well, your friend is a very smart lady. As far as I can tell, her plan was first to make the point that America could control Lebanon, and then to concede Lebanon to Syria in exchange for Syrian partnership on other issues, such as Israel and Iran."

"Why does Syria care about Lebanon?"

"Money and a port, for economic factors, but they have long regarded Lebanon as part of Greater Syria. The Lebanon was originally a district of Syria, but it had been taken away from them by a treaty between European powers. Of course, they feel the same way about Israel, but they'd be willing to recant their claim to Israel in exchange for control of Lebanon."

"Is Lebanon ours to give away?"

"Apparently not. That's what the Amal was saying when they took your friend. The religious, military and business interests all have claims."

"And Brian?"

"Mr. Bowman serves his family's interests. If Syria takes over Lebanon, the Bowmans, the Gamayels, the Hamadis and the other clans will have to strike a bargain with them—and the Syrians are notoriously hard bargainers. A weak national authority allows the families the most freedom to pursue their business."

"Hashish."

"You've been listening to the State Department. Yes, hashish, among other things."

"But what's this nationalistic stuff going on now?"

"The clans see that a strong national government—controlled by themselves—is better than Syria, but not as good as no government. They can't have no government anymore, so they go for the next step."

"So Brian's behind this now?"

"I'm sure the Bowmans have worked out something."

"Why did he help me?"

"Look at it this way. The Amal, which is supported by Iran, took the girl so that the US would not forget them in the negotiations. Without the girl, Iran and the Amal feared they might lose all their status in Lebanon. Without the girl, they would have to join with someone else to defend their claims. It could be anyone else, as long as it wasn't Syria. The Bowmans knew that the Syrians knew that they would have to deal with the families, but the Syrians also felt the factions were so small and divided they could either smash them or integrate them. You freeing the girl made them doubt their assumptions. Syria, acknowledging it couldn't control the independent Lebanese factions, breaks off negotiations. The General comes home empty-handed, and the families accept Iran's help to strengthen the central government. It's a very big shake-up, or shakedown, can't say which."

"So I blew the game for the home team."

"Not really. Lebanon was never ours to concede to Syria in the first place. The premise of the negotiations was wrong, and the deal would have blown up anyway. That's the myopia of the Defense Department, though. They think we own everything, or ought to. You see the way that Colonel treated you. He owned your driver. He thinks he owns it all."

"So the Defense Department thinks I scotched everything."

"I'd bet they do."

"Great!" I was thinking of Elizabeth.

Nusanti was not. "They're not the worst enemy to have, you know. Many people do well without armies behind them."

93.

The funeral had more festivity than mourning, not because people were singing 'Ding! Dong! The Witch is Dead!' but because of all the news about me. So many people showed up to the church that they had to rig some quick speakers for the crowd outside. I said one or two things, just a couple of memories of going to ball games and honoring my mother for keeping the marriage together. Most of the people who were there either didn't really know my father, or knew that he was a violent and difficult drunk who died like a beggar, and so I figured that people arrived for the pageant of it, the new hero toasting his roots.

The only conversation I remember was with my dad's old boss, Mr. Hamlin. He pulled me aside during the receiving line. "I've got it set up so that your mother will receive pension benefits just like your dad retired. You know she's been getting his check all along."

"Is it enough for her?"

"With the life insurance policy? Sure."

"What life insurance policy?"

"I know drunks," Irv told me. "They think they'll live forever, but they live shorter even than poor people. Years ago, I got your father to sign on a policy and we've been taking his premium out of his check. It should come to a hundred thousand dollars more or less. Your mother's the beneficiary."

"I can't thank you enough."

"It's a savage world," he told me. "You ought to know that. The most we can do is protect the little part we come in contact with."

"I didn't do much of a job protecting my father."

"How could you? I wasn't protecting your father. I was protecting you and your mother. Like you were protecting that girl of yours."

"If I'd protected her," I told him, "I never would have let her go."

94.

Days spread into one another. Word had gotten to the press that an agent representing my interests had arranged an exclusive interview with *Life,* so the rest of the press backed off. My mother went through patches of incredible pride at her own survival and my accomplishment, and then unrelievable sorrow at having lost her man and at the same time having lost most her life to him. I could only stand by her, that's all I could do. Seems like so little.

I expected that just being in the house would scrape up painful memories, but it didn't. The memories floated up slowly, rose and fell like tide, like seasons. Even the tough times, when my father behaved with unpredictable violence, bloomed in muted colors. The pastels didn't absolve him, I don't mean that, but seeing who I had become, I could forgive him for what he had done to me, to our family. To thank him for making me went beyond reason; but at least I could forgive him for it.

I called Elizabeth to tell her how I felt, but I could hear the patience in her voice.

"Maybe we can end this taboo on talking about our families," I told her. "Maybe it's time."

"What taboo?"

"You know, your family goes your way, mine goes mine. That's how it's been and I'm not sure I like it."

"I guess that's just the way it fell out. They never had much in common."

I took the opening. "Well maybe you can explain something about what your father said to me in New York."

"I don't know. If you have any questions, maybe you should ask him."

"He was very supportive, said he owed me a great debt and that I could ask him for anything."

"He does. I do too."

"But he wanted me to ask his lawyer if I wanted something, not him."

"It's hard to be in debt, like that anyway."

"That's what he said."

"Then that's your answer."

"I just don't get it. Why did he send me over there if he couldn't deal with me coming back?"

I could hear her voice hesitating even as she spoke. "Maybe he didn't expect you to succeed."

So I stayed in Cleveland for longer than I thought I would. My agent called every day with an update on negotiations, and Jim called with love and reports on the vagrant Control Tower. He'd found one swarm from the hive and installed them back into the Control Tower, with mixed results. Some of the bees from each half fought.

Worse news: because the brood received uneven care and feeding during the shortage, there were a huge number of weak and deformed newborns. Bees are savage with their imperfect hive-mates. Bees brook no physical imperfection in their sisters, no wounds, no scars, no missing parts. It's gruesome watching what happens to them, whether it's mutants, or workers wounded in battle, or even with the drones come fall, when the hive decides they won't need any more males. The whole hive bands together to weed out inferior stock. They tear at the legs and wings of their victims with their mandibles until the inferior bees have no fight in them. They drop the wounded bees out of the hive for the birds to eat. Doubtful survival for the Control Tower. Clearly we were going to have to rename the hive when I got back.

I gave a speech at my old high school. My old football coach, who was the vice principal now, called to ask me, and I couldn't tell him no. But the kids were great, really thrilled to meet me. I told them to work hard and to do with conviction even the things you feel you have to do. There's something about talking directly to your past that grows you up in ways years never can. Maybe high school reunions are plots by older generations just to make people grow, to force time's changes out into the bright light. I mean changes other than fat and wrinkles, changes you can wear with pride.

I felt adult going back home again, a feeling I hadn't had before. I suppose the reason I hardly ever went back before was that, the times I did, I felt the way I felt when I lived there, reduced to the mercy of my father's demons. This time back, I brought my own. I took care of my mother, took care of myself, even took care of the kids who were repeating my own experiences. I felt my years and revered every one of them. I'm certain that helped me keep it together when I saw the scene back in DC.

95.

I'd been gone a week and talked to Elizabeth every day, but she hadn't told me about the changes she'd made. She was at work when I landed, so I took a cab from the airport. I was recovering still, plagued by small pains and exhaustion, but renewed by the self my journey backward revealed. I wanted a warm bed, and a warm body in it, but I could wait for the body.

The bed had to wait too, though. The apartment was boxes, not a lot of them, but enough to realize that Elizabeth had spent some time filling them. Most of the bookshelves were empty; most of the books were hers. The bedroom smelled of women's clothes. Several tall closet-boxes stood in a corner. I knew what she had in them, and I knew what she was doing. She was leaving me. Elizabeth was leaving.

I called her, but she couldn't, or wouldn't, come to the phone. I didn't have the physical resources for rage, but I had the personal ones for patience. No matter. What else could I do but wait for her return and wonder what she thought she was up to?

"It's not you, Ron. It's me." We were finally together, finally alone. "This past month has been insane, first with the Lebanon-Syria action and then being taken hostage. Now everyone wants to have a piece of me, the press, the Pentagon, the State Department, you. It's like being take hostage again. I just can't handle it."

"So we'll go away. You don't have to handle all of it. We'll go to an island somewhere, change our names and just disappear for a while."

"I can't. There's a new initiative in the Middle East, and

they want me at the UN to talk it up and strategize. I can hide in New York, just do my work and disappear."

"But what about me? What about us?"

"Don't make this hard."

"Me make it hard? You're the one who's leaving! I'm coming home!"

"I'm going home, too."

"What do you mean?"

"My dad is so lonely. I could tell when he came to Israel, and I've been talking to him. At least I can be around for him."

"And who's going to be around for me? My father?"

"Don't do that! That's awful!"

"Well, who is? What's so awful?"

"It was your father's death that made me realize this was something I had to do. I can't just let my father slip away. He's slipping already, and I can't let it happen."

"But you can let me just slip away."

"For a while, yes."

"What do you mean, a while?"

"Just because I'm moving to New York doesn't mean we're ending it."

I glanced at a cardboard box. The red logo blurred to THE END IS UP in my teary eyes. "Looks like the end to me."

"This isn't permanent. I'm not breaking off with you. New York's not that far away, you know."

"So you couldn't have waited until I got home? Couldn't talk to me about this? It's all up to you? Your choice?"

"I don't want you to try to talk me out of this. I have to get away for a little while. Nothing else is going to be there later: the work, my dad. But you will—"

"I will what?"

"Be there, I hope."

"So, what if I move to New York with you?"

"No."

"No what?"

"I can't live with you right now."

"You are living with me. You have been living with me."

"I love you, Ron, but I owe you my life. You have no idea how hard that is to live with."

"You're right. I have no idea. I can't think, I don't understand. I never have and I never will."

She kissed me then, deep and dark as a well, and took me to bed. It was like that first time, like we were hiding in a deep, dark well from all the militias and deaths and disappointments the world can throw at you. We dove naked into one another at the bottom of that well, mindless of everything, mindless even that one of the dangers flying overhead could land on top of the well, that we might be trapped in its lightless water, apart together forever. I held Elizabeth closer to me than I ever had before, and in my imagination we were hiding out in Elizabeth's lightless room in Dahya, in profound night, a secret from all the battles around us.

96.

I did go to New York to visit three weeks later. Elizabeth called me—she'd been calling me more than I'd been calling her—to say people in New York wanted to meet me and there was a party and could I come.

I felt uncomfortable in my best suit, holding my drink left-handed and hiding my injured right behind me all evening. I could see the dollar signs in the drape of the fabric both the men and women wore. Very few of the guests were American, but I still recognized expensive accents in everyone's mouth.

Everyone recognized me. They came to pass on their congratulations, but most of the honors and sympathy went to Elizabeth. Few people had more to say to me than "Great job!" or "Big, aren't you?"

To Elizabeth, though, they opened conversation. "Has it been awful to adjust after such a harrowing experience?" a grey and wrinkled French woman asked.

"I've seen your father," an Indian man said. Elizabeth explained later he was some species of royalty. "He seems a changed man since your release, and changed for the better."

I did nothing all evening but accompany Elizabeth, reprising my role as her protector. My hands were a nuisance to me. I could tell I wasn't supposed to touch her, but I couldn't tell what else I might do with them and not be judged barbarian. The bandage on my ear marked me as a thug, and I felt like one all evening.

I didn't feel much better back at the apartment. Elizabeth had moved into the one on the Upper East Side, where I had stayed a month before. It looked the same as it did then, except for her clothes and books here and there. I still tired easily and went directly from my suit to the bed. Elizabeth took off nothing but her shoes. "I'm not tired yet," she told me, "and I have work to do." She kissed my forehead and turned the light off. I didn't even have enough strength left to stew in the dark.

But I woke an hour or so later, perhaps from the strangeness of the place. The light was on in the wood-paneled den. I threaded my way barefoot through the street-lighted living room and hallway. Elizabeth sat asleep at the desk, a green glass light shining on her hair, which splayed over the book open under her head.

I tiptoed over, so I could wake her gently with my

touch, but then I saw what the book was: fabric samples, upholstery fabric. She planned to recover the furniture, re-design the apartment in New York, make it her own. I shut off the light and picked my way back to bed alone.

I'm not hurrying back to New York and, though she still calls, I don't think Elizabeth lets me know when she's in DC.

97.

A month has passed since that party in New York. My hearing has returned a bit, and all my wounds have mostly healed over. The left side of my face and neck is not nearly so ragged as I pictured it, though I think it still frightens little children. My ear reminds Jim of some magazine photos of ritually scarred African tribes, almost picturesque. I can't do anything about my face, of course, so I'm learning to wear it proudly.

Jim and I did rename the Control Tower. I leaned to Dahya or Beirut for a while, but after Jim captured another swarm and returned it to the super, he called the hive the Mutant from Outer Space, and the name stuck. I'm beginning to look at bees like creatures from outer space, or from someplace or time further away than any human being will ever reach. Bees haven't changed, physiologically, in a million years or so; that's why you can find rocks with bees encased in them. But they also don't seem to have the capacity for change, either, as if they just dropped down from somewhere and got stuck. But people, we change all the time, sometimes so fast you can't keep up. I mean, Jim's talking about getting married to this new girl, and though I know it's only hormones for now, one of these days, that kind of chemistry will happen in real life.

I haven't gone back to the Census Bureau yet, and I don't know when I will. I'm on medical leave, but I'm still working, keeping myself entertained by the offers people have been making me. Colonel Harbison himself called and wanted to know if I had any interest in a career in anti-terrorism. The offer I liked best came from my father's company, at the headquarters in Cleveland. I'm waiting for inspiration.

Inspiration might have just arrived in the form of Andrea Kowalski. After the evacuation she had to spend a few weeks debriefing in Germany. Now she's back in Washington and called. She wants to see me and she has my packet—the $190,000 I took out of the bank in Beirut. Elizabeth's father never questioned what became of the half-million he gave me for Elizabeth's ransom. Maybe he figures I paid it to free her. And maybe I did. In any case, I already lost the lawyer's card Roger gave me, and I can't see calling him or Elizabeth for another one. I still don't know what I'm going to do with the ransom money, or with the advances and royalties my agent keeps promising me from this deal and that. Maybe buy some more land for Jim to farm and just live out that way with him.

I get the feeling Andrea might be staying in Washington for a while.

The shape of life always mystifies me. No one seems to have any better idea than anyone else how it's supposed to be lived. Some people shape their lives into crosses and others into stars or scythes. Some people—like me, I guess—choose something alive. We make totems of our pets, or our families, or our lovers. I chose bees for my totem, and their powerful wings carried me across a giant portion of my life. Football did that for me before, and fear of my father before that. But now, bees are just mutants from outer space, and I don't know what will carry me from here. I've had the thought that I can go it alone for a while, just shape my life by the shape it takes. It used to enrage me that life came with no rule book, no place you could turn to answer even the easy questions. Now that it appears that even the answers are questions, I'm relieved.

Andrea's on her way over to the apartment now; Elizabeth lets me stay for the same rent I paid before. I think both Andrea and I wonder if we misplaced our trust because of the heat of Beirut. Now it's early July and just as hot in Washington, and regardless of my wondering, I will take Andrea out to the tropical warmth of Jim's farm. There the three of us, and maybe Jim's friend too, will sit in the copse on the Adirondack chairs, drinking gin-and-tonics, and sweat rivulets in the setting sun. I will breathe in the smell of return—to earth, to health, to home, to self—and listen to the gathering quiet of bees settling in for the night.